KT-148-412

HIDDEN DANGER

Faith had only been working at Moonlight Cosmetics for a short time when she was sent to Malta to finalise a contract. On arrival, the car that was to take her to her hotel failed to turn up and she was offered a lift by Hannibal Price, who worked for a local hospitality company. He warned Faith to be wary of Jean-Baptiste Laval, the man she had come to see. Then, when she met Laval the next day, he told her to be careful of Hannibal Price. But which man could Faith trust — and what were both men so desperate to hide?

Books by Brenda Lacey
in the Linford Romance Library:

HIDDEN IDENTITY

BRENDA LACEY

HIDDEN DANGER

Complete and Unabridged

LINFORD
Leicester

First published in Great Britain

First Linford Edition
published 2001

British Library CIP Data

Lacey, Brenda
    Hidden danger.—Large print ed.—
    Linford romance library
    1. Love stories
    2. Large type books
    I. Title
    823.9'14 [F]

    ISBN 0–7089–9739–2

Published by
F. A. Thorpe (Publishing)
Anstey, Leicestershire

Set by Words & Graphics Ltd.
Anstey, Leicestershire
Printed and bound in Great Britain by
T. J. International Ltd., Padstow, Cornwall

This book is printed on acid-free paper

1

Malta was hot. Much hotter than Faith had expected. She had done no more than set one foot outside the airport terminal, and already she was aware of the heat bouncing back at her from the Tarmac. She must have been mad, she thought irritably, to agree to come on this assignment.

There hadn't been much time to think about it. It should have been Stephanie, the chief Sales Executive from Moonlight Cosmetics, standing here today, but she was in hospital recovering from appendicitis.

Faith had received a call late on Friday night, and by Monday morning, here she was. There hadn't even been time to call into the office and pick up the special presentation pack Stephanie had apparently prepared.

'You'll be fine,' Brenda, the Managing Director, had said. 'Stephanie has been there a dozen times. Everything is booked — plane tickets, hotel, exactly as it always is. And don't worry about the presentation pack — you've got your own promotional material. I'm sure it's just as good. Stephanie is just a perfectionist. She always has a hire care waiting at the airport. There will be probably be a map in it, so you have nothing to worry about.'

Except that there was no car. Faith had tried the rental desk. She had been to airport information. She had even come out into the heat and walked the length of the carparks. Nothing. Even the taxi drivers, who had clustered around when the plane landed an hour ago, had found their fares and left. Faith was beginning to wish that she had not dismissed them so loftily. Her appointment with Mr Laval at Sleima was at three fifteen. It was already two o'clock. She would have to do something.

She gave an exasperated sigh. It was all turning out exactly as Charles had said it would.

'Fay, my dear girl,' he had said when she told him, 'that little company of yours may produce wonderful cosmetics, but they couldn't organise their way out of a paper bag. You can't really be going to Malta, just like that. It will be one problem after another. You mark my words!'

Damn Charles! Why was he always right? Well, she told herself firmly, she would not ring and ask his advice. Life was difficult enough without listening to Charles saying pointedly, 'I told you so.'

Not that she wasn't tempted. Charles would know someone, pull a few strings, and everything would go like clockwork. And he had told her to telephone if there was any problem at all.

No, she thought to herself firmly. That was absurd. She could manage perfectly well without Charles Chatcombe. Just because she didn't have everything planned down to the last detail like he did, it didn't mean that she couldn't cope. She wasn't completely useless, otherwise Moonlight Cosmetics would not have offered her this overseas assignment.

He had tried to talk her out of it. 'Fay, darling,' he had said, as they sat at the best table in Charles's favourite restaurant and waited for the lobster and strawberries, 'have you any idea what you are letting yourself in for? You have never been farther than the Isle of Wight in your entire life.'

'Well,' Faith said stoutly, 'this is a golden opportunity.'

Charles gave that little laugh of his which let you know that he thought you an imbecile. 'You think so? It seems absurd to me. Stephanie goes sick at the eleventh hour with a big contract at stake, and do they have another senior executive to take her place? No. Instead they ask you — at all of three days'

4

notice. Junior sales executive? You haven't been in the place five minutes.'

Faith toyed with her lobster. She didn't really care for shellfish.

'Well, they must think I have promise.'

Charles smiled. 'Or, of course, Stephanie may have the whole contract sewn up already, so it is just a question of getting Laval to sign the paper-work. Yes, I expect that is what it is. Still, the way the firm operates, don't be surprised to get there and find that they have forgotten to warn Laval that you are coming.'

He reached out and took her hands in his own, firm, well-manicured ones.

'If you want to go to Malta, why don't you agree to marry me, and we can go together? A honeymoon. Malta, Greece, Italy — we could take in Switzerland on the way back.'

Why did the prospect leave her so cold? Thousands of women would be delighted to share their lives with Charles Chatcombe. And he was genuinely fond of her. Her sister was always urging her to accept him.

'Think about it, Faith. No more money worries. No more nine-to-five.'

But Faith knew the answer. Charles would run her life like he ran his own, as a military operation. No more getting up early to listen to the birds. No more walking on the cliffs because it was raining and the wind was in your face. No more worries. No more excitement . . .

So she had smiled at him, and said, firmly, 'I want to take this job.'

And here she was, hot, late, hungry and irritable, with no car. Well, she would not be beaten. She pulled down the jacket of the fawn, linen suit which had looked so smart and cool in London, and seemed so crumpled now, tossed back her blonde hair and marched back to the Information Desk.

'My car,' she said, knowing that she sounded like an outraged primary school teacher. 'What has happened to my car?'

The pretty girl behind the counter flashed her a patient smile. 'I am sorry, madam. Unless you know the name of the hire company . . . There are many hire firms on the island. But if you wish, I could try and arrange a hire car for you.'

'But it is supposed to have been paid for,' Faith wailed. 'It's a regular thing. I saw the booking form myself.'

'And you don't remember the name of the company?'

Faith shook her head. Last Thursday it hadn't mattered to her.

'Credit card?' the girl said.

Faith shook her head. 'Everything was supposed to be prepaid. And I haven't even brought very much money. I was only supposed to be here for a day or two. And even the taxis have gone, now. I don't know what to do. I've got an appointment in Sleima in less than an hour.'

'Perhaps I can help,' a warm, amused voice said.

Faith spun around. There was a man

at her elbow. He was dark, olive-skinned, with flashing, brown eyes and an easy grace she had already noticed admiringly among some of the young taxi drivers and airport employees. In fact, she thought, she recognised the man. Hadn't he been standing among the taxi drivers touting for custom at the door? Her eyes had been drawn, even then, by the muscular physique under the open-necked shirt.

'My company is supposed to have arranged for a hire car to meet me,' she said. 'But it doesn't seem to have arrived.'

'You have a company?' A smile twinkled at the corners of his eyes.

Was he teasing her? It was impossible to tell. She tossed her head back with what she hoped was an authoritative gesture and said, 'Moonlight Cosmetics. I have an appointment to meet a Mr Laval in Sleima this afternoon — he's a big importer. Not that I suppose you have ever heard of him.'

The brown eyes were as unfathomable as ever.

'Oh, yes. I've heard of him. Malta is a small place. He's an important man, a big importer, as you say. Oh, yes, I've certainly heard of Mr Laval.'

There was something in his tone which made her say, 'And you don't like what you hear?'

He gave a half-comic grin, spreading his hands in a little gesture of deprecation. 'No, no. That is too strong. It is only that we are not alike, he and I. He is a businessman — he thinks only of his work, of profit.'

'And you?'

'Ah, Miss Worthing, I am a creature of sun and sea. I have to make a living, yes, but I work to live — he lives to work. But I am working this afternoon, and maybe, after all, I can be of assistance. I myself am going to Sleima — perhaps I can give you a lift?'

But she was staring at him doubtfully. 'How did you know my name?'

For a moment a faint flush touched

his cheeks, and he shifted his gaze.

'A moment ago,' she persisted, 'you called me Miss Worthing. How did you know my name?'

He shrugged, a little abashed. 'If you do not wish people to use your name, Miss Faith Worthing, you should not write it across your luggage.'

It was her turn to blush. She had completely forgotten the lettering which Charles had insisted on painting across her suitcase. 'I'm sorry, Mr . . . ?'

There was a momentary hesitation. 'Price,' the man said, 'Hannibal Price. How do you do?' He held out his hand. It was warm, tanned and strong, and it enveloped Faith's easily. 'And now that we have been properly introduced, what about that lift to Sleima?'

'How much will it be?' she asked.

He stared at her puzzled. 'How much . . . ?'

She looked at him again. How could she have been such a fool. This man was no taxi-driver. That shirt might be casual, but it was silk. And his watch was a Rolex.

'You are not a taxi-driver?' she stuttered. 'Only I thought I had seen you, when the plane came in, over by the pick up point.'

'Perhaps you did. But I am not a taxi-driver. I am personnel and hospitality manager for a local leisure firm. I came to meet someone — an overseas representative, for my company, but it seems there has been a change of plan.' He picked up her suitcase, and said lightly, 'Which is how I come to be here, heaven sent to aid you. I have a car going to Sleima, and no passenger. You are a passenger going to Sleima without a car — what could be more convenient?'

She hesitated. What would Charles say, she thought. Driving off into the Maltese afternoon with a man she had hardly met.

He seemed to read her thoughts. 'I assure you, Miss Worthing. Your virtue is safe with me.'

It was her turn to blush, a deep

embarrassed red. But she kept her voice steady. 'In that case, Mr Hannibal Price, personnel and hospitality manager. I should be very much obliged.'

Her virtue might be safe with Hannibal Price, Faith thought to herself a few minutes later, but she was not at all sure about the rest of her.

The traffic on the roads was heavy, and even to Faith, accustomed to the disciplined chaos of London, the ride was hair-raising. Trucks lumbered along the highway, ancient buses roared and growled, crawling up the inclines and lurching headlong down the other side in the middle of the road, horns blaring, overtaking everything in their path. Cars which had been built before Faith was born still limped along the dual carriageways, held together with unpainted fibreglass and pieces of string.

Yet, through it all, Hannibal Price drove with careless ease, one hand on the wheel, the other on the horn.

The streets in town were so narrow

that Faith found herself holding her breath, and drawing herself into the smallest possible space, as though somehow that would make it easier for the car to pass between the buildings which scraped by, inches from the windows.

She caught Hannibal's amused glance and knew that he was aware of her reaction. 'Interesting place, Malta,' she said, feeling the need to say something.

He nodded, obviously pleased. 'A lovely island. Melita the Romans called it. Or was it the Greeks? The island of honey.'

'The Romans? I didn't know they were here.'

'Oh, yes. Phoenicians, Arabs, Greeks, Romans, they've all owned Malta. This was where Hannibal's son ceded the Carthaginian empire to the Romans. Hence my name. There are still a lot of Hannibals in Malta.' He steered the car on to the pavement to allow a van to pass. Neither vehicle slowed down.

'The Romans built the roads, I daresay — and they haven't been touched since,' Faith said bitterly, as they lurched back on to a main thoroughfare, over a pile of rubble.

'Perhaps it is as well, after all, that there was no car for you at the airport. The roads are difficult, and it can be hard to find your way on your first day. Maybe, after all, it is better to be driven. Certainly it is a pleasure for me.'

Did no-one believe she could do anything? She said, rather sharply, 'It would be more of a pleasure for me if you kept your eyes and mind on the road, instead of giving me history lessons.'

Hannibal said nothing, but drove on in silence, his face steely. His driving was no longer relaxed, but precise, calculated, and much, much too fast. At least, it would have been too fast if it had been less skilful. For he was, she suddenly realised, a superb driver.

'Yes,' she said, breathlessly, as they turned into a wide and beautiful boulevard which fronted the sea, 'you make your point. You drive superbly when you care to.'

His response surprised her. The grimness left his face, and he smiled — a genuine smile of pleasure. 'Thank you — that was generous, Miss Worthing. I did not deserve it. I was trying to alarm you.'

She grinned back. 'Call me Faith.'

'Friends?'

She nodded. 'Friends.'

'In that case,' he said lightly, 'what about meeting me for a drink after your meeting with Mr Laval? I'll pick you up at your hotel. In fact, I'll do better than that. It's ten past three now, so if you are meeting him at quarter past you certainly won't have time to go to your hotel first. Why don't I drop you at Import International, and take your luggage to the Cranmore? It will save you worrying about it. Then I'll pick you up there later. Wouldn't that be a good idea?'

She had already been worrying about what to do with her luggage. It would have been embarrassing turning up to a business meeting with her suitcase under her arm.

'That would be very helpful. I have everything I need with me.'

He grinned. 'Great. Well, we're here. Import International. I'll drop you off at the front, if you don't mind. I'd rather not be seen here — as I told you, Laval and I don't see eye to eye.'

He drew up outside a large, modern building, set back a little from the road. A little fountain played in the court-yard. Through the huge, plate-glass doors, Faith could just see a cool foyer in white and green marble, with a flight of stone stairs arching up to a graceful balcony.

'Go on then,' Hannibal urged. 'You only have a minute or two.'

Faith seized her briefcase and was in the act of opening the car door, but a sudden thought stopped her.

'How did you know the time of my appointment? Quarter past three you said. I didn't say anything about the time I was due to meet Laval.'

Hannibal laughed. 'You are a suspicious creature. You were telling the girl at Airport Information when I arrived. Don't you remember?'

'Of course.' She smiled, feeling rather foolish. 'How silly! I don't know what has got into me. I've been feeling over-anxious ever since I arrived.'

He grinned. 'That's natural. This whole business of the car is upsetting. No, don't worry about it. You just go and see Mr Laval. I'm sure he'll be able to arrange transport back to your hotel. I'll deliver your suitcase, and see you later.'

She nodded, and got out of the car. 'Thanks. Seven o'clock OK?'

'Seven o'clock is fine. Now, good luck with your meeting. And, Faith — '

'Yes?'

'Do you know Laval?'

She shook her head. 'Never met him. Why?'

He looked at her for a long moment. 'Just be careful, that's all.'

She stopped in the act of closing the car door. 'What do you mean?'

He shrugged, avoiding her gaze. 'Oh, you know what these older men are. Probably nothing to worry about. See you at the Cranmore. Seven o'clock.'

And he was gone. Faith stood for a moment gazing after the car. What had he meant by saying that about Laval?

And then, like a cold trickle down her spine, another thought struck her. Her luggage might have told him her name. She might have told the girl at the airport the time of her appointment with Laval. But she was absolutely certain that never, at any moment, had there been any mention of the Hotel Cranmore.

Who, or what, was Hannibal Price? And why, oh why, had she allowed him to drive away with her luggage?

'Miss Worthing? I have been expecting you.' A man was standing at the open door of Import International, a quizzical look on his face. 'Welcome to Malta. I am Jean-Baptiste Laval . . . '

2

As they made their way into the building, Faith could not help remembering Hannibal's words of warning.

Why should she be careful? Was it Laval's reputation with the ladies? Certainly he moved and spoke like a man who thought himself attractive. He was around fifty years old, dark and good-looking for a man his age, but there was a hint of sensuality in the way he squeezed her hand, and more than a little vanity in the way in which he straightened his hair as they passed the long, gilded mirrors at the top of the stairs.

But he was clearly a powerful man. Some women were attracted by that. Faith noticed the respect with which the little receptionist received his greeting as they passed, and the speed with which the young security man

20

leaped up to open the door. Jean-Baptiste Laval was obviously a man to be reckoned with.

The room into which he led the way was luxurious in the grand style. Her feet sank into the deep-pile carpets, as he led her across to the two sofas nestling under potted plants in a corner. In the centre of the room was an artificial fountain, where a statue of a naked Cupid watered lilies in a marble pool.

Laval followed her gaze. 'Nice little thing, isn't it? I picked it up on one of my trips abroad. Creates a nice atmosphere in the office, don't you think?' His English was perfect, without a trace of accent.

'Now,' Laval said, settling himself on one of the sofas, and gesturing her to the other. 'I was sorry to hear about your — Stephanie is she called? I hope she will soon recover. Now, we have a lot to talk about, I think.'

Faith took a deep breath. This was

what she had been waiting for, and she had spent a lot of time preparing her sales-pitch, as Charles called it.

'Yes,' she said, 'Moonlight Cosmetics has brought out a new product range especially with the Mediterranean market in mind. Cool, seductive, sweet, but not cloying.' She pulled out one of the tiny samples from her briefcase and opened it to release the perfume. 'Mediterranean Moonlight, a wholly new and sensual experience . . . ' She settled down to give the sales talk of her life.

She could see that he was interested, almost from the first. And he was demanding. Faith began to see why Stephanie had taken the trouble to prepare a special presentation pack for him. As the discussion went on, she began to wish that she had taken the time to collect it. This man controlled the import market to the eastern Mediterranean, and he knew what he wanted.

He wanted samples, for one thing.

Faith gave him several of her mini-phials, but he was contemptuous. 'Toilet water,' he said. 'It is very pretty, but the serious money is in the real perfume. You have none of that?'

'I could arrange it,' she said, hedging. If there was a Fax machine at the hotel she could ask Brenda to send something on the next plane.

Laval was turning the publicity material over and over in his hands as if he was looking for something which he could not find.

'I shall need more information than this,' he said. 'You don't have any other documentation? No Maltese translations, or anything like that?'

Faith frowned. Why, she wondered, did Laval, whose command of English was so perfect, require a Maltese translation to understand the proposition Moonlight was making to him.

'No,' she said positively. 'What you see here is everything I have. Stephanie had prepared a special pack for you, but I stepped in at the last moment, and I don't have it. But, frankly, there was nothing there that I have not told you, except more information about publicity and presentation materials. Posters, bottles, labels for the Mediterranean market — that sort of thing.'

Laval gave her a cool smile. 'My dear, young lady, to an importer there are few things more important than publicity. This nothing, as you call it, may make the difference between commercial success and failure. Your Stephanie obviously appreciates that. Perhaps, after all, it would be better to wait before making a decision. You have done the spade work — I'll make a final decision when I have had a chance to talk to your colleague.'

He went to the desk and picked up the phone.

It was like a slap in the face. As suddenly as that, it seemed, Laval had lost interest in the product. She realised that she had handled it badly, and began to say quickly, 'I've got some of the British publicity material back at the hotel. Perhaps we could arrange another meeting. Brenda could Fax the information, and organise the samples that you want — '

But Laval broke in.

'I think it is better that I deal directly with Stephanie. After all, she does have a knowledge of the market. No, don't look so downhearted. It was unlikely that I would buy anything straight away, in any case. The sale of luxury goods is not what it was. Your presentation certainly aroused my interest. I will give this some thought. In the meantime, let me order you some coffee — I'm sure you must be thirsty and worn out after your long flight.'

And that was that. Faith sat, stunned, as he took up the receiver and began to speak. The conversation was in a language she did not understand, and she looked idly around at the cool, spacious office.

Suddenly, though, her attention was drawn to him. 'Cranmore.' It sounded exactly as if, in the midst of that stream of unintelligible speech, Laval had said the word Cranmore.

She glanced at him sharply, and he gave her a warm, supportive smile.

I'm being absurd, she thought. He was expecting Stephanie. It was her hotel booking — obviously he is discussing the change of plan. What could be more natural? She smiled back wanly.

He put down the phone and returned to her side, smiling warmly.

'My receptionist,' he explained. 'Just asked her to send some coffee and biscuits.'

Coffee did arrive, strangely bitter coffee, and a plate of delicious, little, almond biscuits, brought in on a tray by the receptionist. But Laval seemed reluctant to bring the meeting to an end, pressing her to more and more coffee, and asking a thousand questions about Moonlight Cosmetics and what he called the fragrance scene in Europe — most of which Faith was totally unable to answer.

She was beginning to wonder whether this protracted conversation was because Laval was taking a personal interest in her or, more prosaically, whether she was expected to offer him better terms, but she was not empowered to do that. She was saved from this anxiety, however, by the telephone, which rang shrilly.

Laval answered it, again in that foreign tongue. The conversation was very short, and as he put down the receiver, he turned to her with an engaging smile.

'Another appointment, I regret to say. I had quite forgotten. Well, it has been nice to meet you, Miss Worthing. And please do not concern yourself. I will, I promise you, reconsider this in a month or two. In the meantime, you have a day or two to enjoy the island. And just to prove there are no hard feelings, won't you let me take you to dinner?'

There was nothing she wanted to do less. In other circumstances it might have been difficult to refuse, since the man still was an important client, but this time she had the perfect excuse.

'I'm sorry,' she said, 'but I've promised to meet someone this evening.'

Laval stiffened. The sudden tension in him was obvious, and his voice was carefully calm as he said, too casually, 'You know someone on the island? Is it anyone I know?' It sounded pressing, and he must have felt it, because he said, with a laugh, 'Malta is a very small island.'

Well, she would not satisfy his curiosity. 'Oh, I doubt it. Just someone I met at the airport. There had been a mix-up over the hire car, and this young man gave me a lift, that's all.'

Laval stared at her. 'You got a lift?'

He sounded outraged, as though it were a personal affront. Just like Charles, she thought, and she returned, rather acidly, 'Is that so surprising?'

Laval pulled himself together with an obvious effort. 'No, no, of course not.

Very fortunate, in fact. I was merely thinking how unfortunate it was to find that there was no car to meet you in the first place. And you will, of course, have no transport to your hotel. Do allow me to find you a taxi — or offer you a lift, indeed. Under the circumstances, that is the least I can do.'

The heat outside was shocking in its intensity, and the noise and bustle of the street with its jostling people and impatient traffic was a strange contrast to the cool, quiet shade of the room they had just left.

Laval operated an electronic device beside the entrance, and a pair of double shutters flew open. They were so narrow, even in this modern building, that Faith had supposed that they covered a large window, but in fact a small courtyard was revealed. A large, white, executive saloon was parked there. Laval flicked the key at it, and the door catches sprang open. He was like a child, Faith thought, showing off a new toy. It reminded her of Charles.

Laval edged the big, white car out into the road. He said very little as they swerved in and out of the traffic, but every few moments he shot a glance in Faith's direction, as though to ensure that she was duly impressed.

He drove with none of Hannibal's finely-judged finesse. Instead they swerved dangerously between oncoming vehicles. Twice they overtook by mounting the pavement on the wrong side of the road, and more than once they shuddered to a stop only inches from an oncoming car which hooted furiously as it sped past.

'Is driving in Malta always like this?' Faith managed to ask, as they came to a halt in the middle of an intersection.

Laval laughed. 'To drive in Malta you must be assertive, certainly. It is a question of temperament.' He turned the car into a side street so suddenly that the tyres screamed. Faith opened her eyes, and was astonished to see that some of the shops signs were in Arabic.

'Where are we going?' she demanded.

'It is a short cut,' Laval said. 'You're at the Cranmore, aren't you? That is where Stephanie was to stay.'

Faith sighed. 'Yes. That's right.'

Laval negotiated a corner by driving over a pile of bricks. 'Here we are, the Cranmore,' he said, drawing up outside the door of a large, modern hotel. 'I'll see you settled in.'

The appearance of Laval in the hotel foyer had an instantaneous effect. Young men in uniform appeared as if by magic to open doors, offering chairs and drinks, and seized Faith's briefcase with eager hands.

'I'll take this straight up to your room for you, madam. The rest of your luggage is there already. The young man in the black coupé brought it in earlier.'

'Black coupé?' Laval said sharply. 'It wouldn't have been Mr Hannibal Price would it, this young man?'

Now I have done it, Faith thought. Hannibal particularly did not want Laval to know he had been involved in bringing her from the airport.

'Yes,' she said, unwillingly. 'At least, I believe that was his name.'

'You want to be careful of that young man,' Laval said. 'He claims to be a personnel and hospitality manager, these days, so I hear. Hospitality manager! A fancy way of saying that he squires foreign visitors around the island at his firm's expense. Still, nothing about Hannibal Price would surprise me. So treat him with care. Which reminds me. Try to avoid any time-share agents you might meet. They'll try to lure you into their presentations, and sell you time-share apartments. You ought to be warned.'

Faith shot him a glance. 'Why did you suddenly say that? Are you telling me that Hannibal Price is dishonest, too?'

Laval shrugged. 'Keep away from him, that's all I say. And don't tell him too much.'

She sipped the gin and tonic slowly. 'There were one or two things I did wonder about — '

She regretted the words as soon as they were spoken, but Laval said, immediately, 'What things?'

'Oh,' she said, 'I don't know. My name, where I was staying — that sort of thing. Nothing significant. It just seemed a bit odd, that's all.'

'He's obviously been talking to one of his lady friends,' he commented. 'Breaks a lot of hearts, our Mr Price.'

Why did that simple remark make Faith feel so miserable and let down? A thought struck her. 'You think he knows Stephanie?'

There was a little silence. She knew what that meant. She asked, simply, 'How well?'

Laval got to his feet. 'I couldn't altogether tell you that. But, if I'm any judge, I would say he knew her quite well. Certainly well enough to know the name of this hotel. Beware of hospitality managers, Miss Worthing. Perhaps, after all, we shall meet again. After all, we do a lot of business with Moonlight Cosmetics.' He shook her hand firmly.

'It was nice to have met you. Enjoy your stay.'

And that, she thought bitterly as she collected her key and went up the stairs, is what you get for harbouring secret dreams about good-looking, amusing, young men you hardly know. No wonder Hannibal Price had been at the airport. No wonder there had been no car. There never had been a car. It was probable, Faith thought suddenly, that Stephanie never ordered a car, whatever the expense account said about it. There was always Hannibal.

She let herself into her room. Her case was on the bed. Naturally. It was a double room, and Hannibal probably had a key. She sighed. There was a lot she had to learn about human nature. And now she had agreed to meet him for a drink tonight. She heartily wished there was some way she could escape it now.

Well, at least she could freshen up and change her clothes. She went into the bathroom to take a shower, but the sight of the deep tub and the complimentary toiletries changed her mind. She would have a long, relaxing bath instead.

Faith opened her suitcase and began to unpack. She might as well do that while the bath was running.

She took out her shoes and stacked them neatly in the bottom of the wardrobe, and began to hang the dresses. But suddenly she stopped, a hanger in her hand, and came back to the suitcase, frowning.

Something was wrong. The clothes in the case were neatly folded, but they were not as she had packed them. She was sure of that. She had not brought a great deal, but Charles had come over especially to supervise the packing, and the things she had brought had all been arranged in his usual logical order, underwear in one pile, daywear in another, eveningwear, nightwear and swimwear in a third.

Now her swimming costume and nightshirt were amongst her underwear, and her green, silk dress was neatly folded under the sundress. She sat down on the bed and stared at the case.

There was no disguising the fact. Someone had been through her luggage.

3

She had a list, of course. Charles would never have permitted her to set off without a detailed list, for insurance purposes. A quick check showed that nothing was missing. That was a relief.

She could not help feeling cheated and vulnerable, though, at the thought of someone rifling her things. Had it been Hannibal? It was possible, but then she remembered Charles's warnings about hotel thieves. 'They always strike on the first day, that's when tourists have the most to lose. So don't leave your suitcase unattended.' Which, of course, she had. Still, nothing was missing, and under the circumstances there was no point in reporting it.

She removed her crumpled clothing and lowered herself into the perfumed waters of the bath.

It did restore her spirits. True, it had

been a difficult day. One worry after another, just as Charles had predicted. But perhaps, she thought to herself, she had been too ready to panic.

What, after all, had really happened? There had been that business at the airport, Stephanie's secret rendezvous with Hannibal. That had got the day off to a bad start, and Faith had been ready to see mysteries everywhere. She still felt embarrassed when she remembered her challenge to Hannibal over how he knew her name.

True, she had failed to clinch the contract with Laval. But even that was not a total disaster. Laval had virtually promised to place a large order in future. She had not entirely blown it.

All the same, it had not been a very good day. Well, she thought, she had no more work to do in Malta. If Laval was not buying a consignment, there was no need to set up marketing strategies, or talk to freight companies. She simply had three days in Malta, all expenses paid. She might as well enjoy it.

She was in a more positive frame of mind at seven o'clock as she went downstairs into the bar.

Hannibal Price was waiting for her, sitting at a table in the corner. He got up as she come in.

'Shall we go outside?' he said. 'They have a garden bar and a pool. Malta is delightful in the evening.'

He was right. The pool was deserted, but the blue waters rippled in the late sunlight.

'Let me get you a drink, Faith,' he offered as she took her seat. 'What will you have? Gin and tonic? Or something a little more exciting.'

Faith could not suppress a grin. It was so different from being out with Charles. His idea of a drink for her was a dry, white wine. It would never occur to him to suggest anything else. She looked up. Hannibal was regarding her quizzically. It was irresistible. 'Something exciting perhaps,' she said, and, before he could say anything more, added, 'I'll let you choose.'

It was a cocktail, when it came. White and creamy and tasting of coconut, and decorated with cherries and little umbrellas. It was delicious, but, as she soon discovered, it was by no means as innocent as it looked.

'I'll remember that you like that one,' Hannibal said, when she expressed her delight.

Perhaps it was the alcohol, but Faith felt her heart give a little flutter.

'I'll remember that you like it.' That must mean, mustn't it, that she would see him again?

She looked at him, sipping his brandy and smiling gently at her. He had changed his clothes, and the fawn suit and cream shirt showed off his dark skin and glowing eyes to perfection. This man is beautiful, she found herself thinking. Like a work of art. I could look at him for ever.

'How did you get on with Laval?' Hannibal asked.

She pulled herself together sharply. That cocktail must be powerful. She had been staring at him like a moonstruck teenager.

'Not very well. He listened very politely, but he made it clear that he wasn't interested, at least for the present. Odd really. I thought to begin with that he was very interested — kept asking questions and probing, even wanted Maltese translations of everything. Then all of a sudden he changed his mind.'

Hannibal gave her a sympathetic smile.

'Bad luck. I wonder what brought that about?'

'I wondered if I was supposed to offer him special terms, but I can't do that without the OK from London.'

Hannibal made a face. 'Anything's possible. I'm rather surprised he didn't sign, though. I got the impression he — ' He stopped abruptly.

'He what?'

Hannibal turned his brandy glass in his fingers. 'Well, let's just say, he likes to be in on everything. If there's

41

something new, something special — Laval usually wants to get his hands on it. He'd like to have a monopoly, you see.'

'Well, we would have offered him a sole agency,' Faith said. 'And the product is going to be a winner, as you say.' She shrugged. 'Oh, well, some you win . . . I still have a few days to enjoy the island. Let's look at it that way. Here's to Malta.' She downed the remains of the smooth, white liquid.

He raised his own glass matching her mood. 'Will you have another?'

It was tempting. She could feel her inhibitions ebbing away, although whether that was the drink or the sunshine, or the company of this man, she could not altogether tell. A little of all three perhaps. But, she reminded herself firmly, it would not do. Whatever would Charles say?

'No thank you,' she said, in her best, prim voice. 'It has been lovely, truly it has. But now, I really should go and get myself some dinner.'

She stood up.

His reaction surprised her. 'Of course, you haven't eaten. You must be starving. Where would you like to eat?'

It was the last thing she was expecting, and for a moment she protested.

'No, really, I couldn't possibly impose — '

He laughed, a wicked, amused chuckle. 'Really, Faith Worthing, you are enchanting. I love that English properness of yours. You pull yourself up and toss your head and put on a voice like a school teacher and say something very conventional. And all the time I can read the spirit of adventure in your eyes. Of course you are coming out to dinner with me. We should both be very disappointed if you did not. Besides, you are a stranger to the island. You must allow me to show you some of its delights. I'm very good at it. After all, that is what my company employs me to do.'

She stood for a moment undecided.

She was not altogether sure that she enjoyed being spoken to in this manner. It was one thing for Charles to organise her life, but this stranger was a different matter. Why should he blithely assume that she would have dinner with him. There was no 'of course' about it. And yet, some little spirit of devilment urged her it was what she wanted to do. Besides, however scornful Laval had been about it, Hannibal was right. He knew his way around the island. She hesitated.

And like all those who hesitate, she was lost. Hannibal caught her eye, and smiled.

'All right,' she said ungraciously, 'you win. Where shall we go?'

*　*　*

'This place you're taking me to,' Faith said, twenty minutes later, 'where exactly is it?'

She tried to keep her voice neutral, but she was becoming increasingly alarmed. They had left Sleima, and had come out on to what was clearly a country road. It was getting dark now, and the road was deserted. Only the occasional silhouette of a tiny chapel or the irregular dark mass of a prickly pear broke the skyline. How few trees there were on the island, Faith thought, and how few people there seemed to be here.

A car came towards them, headlights lurching over the uneven road. Faith felt a sudden rush of relief at this sign of habitation and realised how uneasy she was becoming.

'Not far now,' Hannibal said, and even as he spoke, they turned a corner and found themselves waiting to join a major road.

'There,' he said, gesturing to the hillside beyond. 'That's where we are going. My favourite place on all the island. Mdina. The silent city.'

Faith looked. There was a city on the hilltop, not large by the look of it, but dominated by a huge dome which glinted silver in the moonlight.

'It looks lovely,' she said, relief and confusion filling her in equal degree.

'It is a fascinating place,' Hannibal said. 'It was the capital of the island, long ago. That dome you can see is the cathedral. It is a cathedral. It shares that honour with another church in the capital.'

'Valetta?' Faith said. 'That is something I was wondering about. Why does a major company like Import International have its offices in Sleima instead of in the capital? There's even a port at Valetta. Doesn't it seem odd to you?'

She looked at Hannibal. In the darkness, he was smiling.

'No,' he said, 'and it would not seem odd to you either if you knew the place. I will take you to Valetta tomorrow, and you will see for yourself.'

She wanted to press him, but he would say no more, and she had to content herself with the thought that, at the least, he had promised to see her tomorrow. She had known him such a short time, and already the idea of spending a day here without seeing him seemed intolerable.

'Tell me about this restaurant,' she said, to cover the silence.

'It's designed for tourists,' he said. 'But I think you will enjoy it.'

'And it is here somewhere?' she said, as the car climbed a steep hill. It was difficult to see in the darkness, but there seemed to be fine houses on the bank, set back among shrubs and bushes. Some were clearly hotels or restaurants.

'No,' Hannibal said equably. 'Our restaurant is in Mdina.' He turned down a little road, and drew the car to a halt under a tall, stone wall. 'Now, this is where we get out and walk.'

He got out, and came around the car to open her door. As he did so, a man appeared from the shadows. Hannibal got out and murmured to him. Faith heard the chink of coins. Her anxiety returned.

'Hop out then,' Hannibal said. 'We

have to walk from here.'

Faith hesitated. 'Where is the restaurant?'

'Through that gate over here,' Hannibal said. 'We're outside the walls of the city. You need a pass to drive in there. Besides, the streets are too narrow.'

Faith squinted through the darkness. She could just make out the dark bulk of the city walls, and the arch that pierced them.

Behind them a car swept in and parked on the other side of the open space, close to the gate. A group of noisy, young people climbed out, laughing and calling to each other in English. They were clearly visitors. While they were locking the car, the shadowy figure edged out of the darkness.

'Got any change, Bill?' one of the tourists shouted. 'I always forget we have to pay the parking attendant.'

Faith was glad of the darkness which covered the glow of her cheeks. What was wrong with her? She was making mysteries out of nothing. She clambered out of the car, and gave Hannibal one of her warmest smiles.

'Ready when you are,' she said.

He looked surprised, but pleased. 'You have relaxed a little, Faith. I'm glad of that. Come and let me show you Mdina, the silent city.'

The little town they came into as they went through the gate almost made Faith exclaim aloud. It was clear why driving on these streets was not encouraged. The houses rose on either side of the street scarcely more than an arm's breadth apart. And it was silent. They could hear the giggles of the young people who had gone in before them, but otherwise the town seemed quiet.

'Dark, isn't it?' she said. It was a strange thing to say, because there were lights, yet the impression of darkness was very strong.

'Yes,' Hannibal said, 'It's the houses, you see. Most of them don't have windows that face the street. That's why they call it the silent city. Everything here is built around courtyards — partly for shade, and partly, I think, because Mdina suffered so much from siege and attack. Houses were very hard for an attacker to get into when there were no windows.'

That was it, of course. That was why the noise — even the occasional burst of singing — was remote, muffled behind the stone walls. That was why the lights shone as pools in surrounding darkness — the lights from the houses made little oases of light which flickered on the tops of courtyard walls, but little of the light fell on the street. All of a sudden Faith's fear evaporated, and she felt the enchantment of the place.

'How lovely,' she breathed, and Hannibal put his arm around her waist.

'I knew you would feel it,' he said. 'You must see the place in daylight, too. Now, down this street, and we shall find our restaurant.'

He led the way through the little labyrinth of lanes. It would be very easy, Faith reflected, to get totally lost in this city, although it was so small. The street they were in seemed to be curving back, so that she was sure that they would end up back at the gate, but when they emerged, at last, into a little square, it was a place she had certainly never seen before.

'Our restaurant,' Hannibal said. 'Set into the city walls. And they do some of the finest Maltese food on the island.'

Indeed it was delicious. Directed by Hannibal, Faith tasted a variety of dishes with a taste and texture she had never encountered before.

'This is wonderful,' she said as she took a mouthful of some exotic fish. 'What is it?' She had some idea of ordering this dish, boldly, the next time Charles took her to his seafood restaurant.

Hannibal's face lit in a grin.

'You like it? Good. I wanted you to taste it before I told you what it was.'

'Tell me,' she said, hardly daring to ask.

'Swordfish.'

For a moment Faith pulled a face, and then reason got the better of her. She had eaten it and it had been delicious. It didn't matter that it was unfamiliar.

'I'll remember that,' she said. 'I'll order it again sometime.'

She could see that she had pleased him. He leaned forward and poured her another glass of wine, and as he did so his hands brushed hers. She felt the little tingle that came from his touch and knew that this night was special.

They ate, laughed, talked and, later, when the orchestra struck up, he took her hand and led her to the tiny dance floor, and they danced. She was not a good dancer, but in his arms she was as light as a feather. It was magical.

But, at last, it was time to return to Sleima. They walked back through the twisting streets in the silent, warm darkness which had become a caress. His arm was around her, and her head nestled on his shoulder as they walked.

At the hotel she half expected him to come in with her, but he did not. He opened the car door for her, and tilting her head back, met her lips in a kiss which set her blood on fire.

'Good-night, Faith,' he said, gently. 'I'll see you tomorrow.'

It was not a question. She nodded.

But before he left her, she had to know the truth about Laval. 'Hannibal?'

He turned to her, his eyes smiling. 'Yes?'

'What exactly is a personnel and hospitality manager?'

He laughed. 'Yes, it sounds very grand, doesn't it? Actually, it isn't. I am responsible for new appointments, of course, but there aren't many of those. Most of the time I act as a sort of guide and entertainments officer to people from overseas — drive them around, tell them about the island. History is my love, you see — and I speak English and Italian. And I've been a manager in the hotel industry, so when the job came up . . . ' He broke off, grinning.

'Have I told you enough?'

How Laval twisted things, Faith thought. But there was one other question . . . 'Hannibal, was it serious, your friendship with — with Miss Ranier? Did you take her to that restaurant?'

He was frowning. 'With whom?'

This time she found the words. 'Stephanie. Stephanie Ranier.'

He looked at her blankly. 'Stephanie Ranier? I've never heard of her. Who on earth is she?' Suddenly his gaze narrowed. 'Is this something Laval told you?'

She nodded. 'He said that you and she were good friends. Very good friends, in fact.'

Hannibal's voice was bitter. 'Oh, he did, did he? Well, if he says so, it must be true. He probably has half-a-dozen computer entries to prove it. Does that satisfy you?'

And with that, he slammed the car door, and was gone.

4

It was very far from satisfying her. Faith stood looking after the car, cold with disappointment and unhappiness. Why had he reacted like that? And why had he begun by lying to her?

Because it must have been a lie. What Laval said made absolute sense. If Stephanie was expecting to meet Hannibal Price, it explained everything. If not, there were a thousand questions to be answered.

She went slowly up to the bedroom and sat down heavily on the bed. Of course Hannibal knew Stephanie. But he had wanted to keep it from her. She didn't have to ask why. Hadn't Laval warned her about trusting Hannibal Price? He was trying to sweep her off her feet — had very nearly succeeded. He was hardly likely to mention his previous conquests. She tried not to remember that during the whole evening of talking to Hannibal about her life in London she had said not a single word about Charles.

It was not the same, she told herself. If he had asked her outright about a man in her life, she would not have denied it. And as for pretending that he had never heard Stephanie's name . . . Why then, had he suddenly changed his mind like that?

She could find no answers to any of her questions. And it was no good sitting here all night worrying over it. She would simply have to ask Hannibal in the morning. She got up and prepared herself for bed.

Sleep on it, she told herself as she switched off the light.

She woke to find the light streaming into her bedroom. But when she threw open the curtains, expecting to find it a bright and cloudless day, she found, instead, that a grey haze curtained the world, echoing her mood.

She felt depressed. Nothing in Malta

had been remotely what she had expected. She showered, changed and went down for breakfast in an unhappy frame of mind.

A little food restored her. There was cereal and fruit, but she declined these, and opted instead for cold ham, cheese and a fresh bread roll, served still warm in a little basket. It was delicious, and so was the coffee. Faith began to feel that she was genuinely abroad and began to plan the day ahead.

She was not at all sure, after the way they had parted, whether Hannibal would fulfil his promise to come and take her to Valetta. No time had been mentioned, and she began to worry about what exactly she should do. There was no point in wasting all day in the hotel if he wasn't coming.

She settled on a compromise. She would go to her room and write a report for Brenda. If Hannibal had not arrived by eleven, she would decide he was not coming and go exploring on her own. Taking a firm decision made her feel better, and she went upstairs and buried herself in her papers.

A tap at the door interrupted her. She looked up with a start — she had been so immersed in her writing that she had quite forgotten her surroundings. She lifted her head to find that the early-morning mist had lifted, and sun was streaming in through the window. Everything was golden and she could hear the laughter and chatter of the sunbathers on the terrace, and the splashing of swimmers in the pool.

She glanced at her watch. It was past ten thirty. That must be Hannibal at the door. He had come after all.

Before she had moved, however, the door opened. A small, dark girl in hotel uniform stood in the doorway, a pile of towels over her arm. She looked at Faith in absolute alarm, blurted out, 'Chambermaid. I'm sorry, madam, I'll come back later,' and scuttled away, slamming the door behind her.

Faith returned to the desk and put away her papers, folding her now complete report neatly, and sliding it between the pages of the sales folder. As she did so she smiled grimly. Her first major assignment had not been an overwhelming success. Well, there was no point in moping about it. She put the folder into the drawer and taking her camera and bag, went out to meet the day.

The little maid was in the corridor pushing a trolley of bedlinen, and as she passed, Faith gave her an encouraging smile.

'You can go in now. I've finished,' she said.

The girl gave her a frightened glance, and darted away into the next room.

Faith raised her eyebrows after the retreating girl. Well, that was what you got for trying to be pleasant. Shame. She was a pretty girl, too. Lovely, thick, curly hair, and dark eyes, like that girl . . . no, wait a moment. It wasn't that. Faith frowned. There was something familiar about that girl. She searched her memory. Where had she seen her?

She couldn't think. It must have been here, she thought to herself. Pull yourself together, you're imagining things again.

But as she got into the lift and went down to the foyer, Faith couldn't rid herself of the feeling that, somewhere, she had seen that face before.

She was still frowning as she handed in her key at the desk. The young man in the bow tie gave her a dazzling smile.

'I've been trying to ring you. There is a gentleman waiting for you in the bar.'

Hannibal! Her heart gave a little lurch, and her feet found wings. She had not realised how much she had hoped to see him. She pushed open the door of the bar, and her eyes searched the room eagerly.

At the window, Jean-Baptiste Laval was waiting for her.

Her face fell. She did not mean it to happen, but she was powerless to prevent it, and she saw by his expression that he had seen, and understood.

'You were not expecting me?'

She flushed. 'I was half-expecting a friend, but there was no firm arrangement. In any case I'd almost given him up.' She rallied enough to flash him a smile. 'What can I do for you, Mr Laval?'

But Laval's mind did not seem to be centred on business. 'I imagine Mr Price has other calls on his time. I did try to warn you, Miss Worthing.'

'There was no firm arrangement — ' she began, and then realised, too late, that she had as good as confessed that the friend was Hannibal Price. She went on swiftly. 'So if there is anything you would like to discuss . . . '

'Discuss? No,' Laval said. 'I think our business was concluded yesterday. But you did mention that you had had problems with car hire. I thought perhaps I could be of service there.'

'Oh, I couldn't possibly impose.'

'No imposition,' Laval said smoothly. 'The car is at the door. There is petrol in the tank. I have left a map for you, marking places of interest. It is a pity for you not to see the island while you are here. Do you have your driving licence?'

'Of course,' Faith said. 'I brought it, supposing there was a car waiting. It is very kind of you to go to all this trouble. But I haven't enough money — it would have to be claimed from Moonlight Cosmetics in London.'

Laval reached over and squeezed her arm in that familiar way of his. He seemed more relaxed, suddenly, more genuinely friendly and warm. She was not sure that she liked it.

'Don't worry, Faith. It is the least I can do, after bringing you all this way, only to disappoint you. You can leave the car at the airport when you leave. I'll see that it is collected. Here is the key. And now, my dear, young lady, I have work to attend to. I hope you enjoy your time on the island.' And he was gone, almost before Faith had time to take in what he had said.

Frowning, she picked up the key

from the table where he had left it. What was Laval playing at? Why should he lend her a car? And what would he expect in return? She pushed open the doors of the bar and hurried out, determined to catch him if she could.

She was too late. Through the open doorway of the hotel she could see him, climbing into the passenger seat of the white, executive saloon she had ridden in the day before. There was a man in the driver's seat, a young man with dark wavy hair. Was it Hannibal? She could not be sure. Laval was saying something with a laugh, and as she watched he closed the door and the car pulled away.

'I hope your conference was satisfactory,' a cool voice said in her ear.

Faith whirled round to face Hannibal, a smile already on her face. But there was no matching pleasure on his. His eyes were steely and his mouth was grim as he said, 'I hope my arrival did not interrupt any delicate negotiations?'

'Arrival? I didn't know you had

arrived. I'd no idea you were here until now.'

'No,' he said, in that same even, cold tone. 'I don't suppose you did. I imagine you thought that when I got your message I would simply go away. Obviously I should have done so, but I thought, just possibly, something real had cropped up, and so I came back. My mistake. I apologise.'

She was staring at him, open-mouthed and motionless in the middle of the doorway, so that an old gentleman with a suitcase had to ask her politely to step out of his way. The little incident jerked her out of herself and she managed to say, 'What are you talking about? What message?'

'You know perfectly well what message,' he said, impatiently. 'The Miss Worthing does not wish to be disturbed, she has urgent business to attend to message. That message!'

He handed her a scrap of paper. She read it, uncomprehending. The words, neatly printed in capital letters, were exactly as he had quoted.

She stared at him. 'Where did you get this?'

'I got it from the reception desk, of course. Where do you think I got it from?'

She looked from him to the piece of paper in her hand. 'Well, who wrote it?'

It was his turn to stare. 'You mean, you didn't? It looks like the writing on your suitcase.'

She shook her head. 'Of course, I didn't. It's nothing like my writing. And the writing on my case was Charles's.'

The flinty look had left his face. 'I wasn't to know that.'

'I just don't understand it.'

'I think I am beginning to understand,' Hannibal said, and the steel was back in his face. 'Someone wanted to avoid my seeing you, wrote the message and left it for me at reception, thinking I would read it and go away. It might have worked, too, only when I heard that you had spent the whole morning writing a report, I wondered if it was a genuine reason, and I came back to find out.'

'Well, I did write a report,' Faith said, with some heat, 'but only because I was waiting for you. But when you hadn't come by eleven, I gave up. I was just going out when they told me there was someone waiting in the bar and it turned out to be Laval. Even then, I hoped it was you.'

'You did?' The brown eyes softened, and then hardened again as he added, 'Charles?'

She found herself smiling. Hannibal was jealous. It gave her a little thrill of pleasure. 'Charles is just . . . hey, wait a minute. How did you know I was writing a report all the morning?'

The brown eyes shifted their gaze momentarily. 'I asked one of the staff,' he said, after a little pause. 'So, I came back, and there you were in the bar with Laval. What was I supposed to think?'

She nodded, slowly. 'Yes, I can see how it looked — how it was meant to look.' She frowned. 'Did he write the note, do you think?'

'It doesn't look like his writing,' Hannibal said, doubtfully.

'Anyway,' Faith said, 'I can't see what he would have to gain by it. It seems an awfully elaborate trick just to spite us.'

'Who else knew you were here?' Hannibal said.

'Not many people. Brenda, Stephanie, Charles — but they're all in England. This note is written on hotel notepaper. Whoever wrote this was certainly here this morning. And you don't think it's Laval's writing.'

Hannibal shook his head slowly. 'He has a very distinctive French script, but is difficult to tell with capital letters. Perhaps that is why the writer used them.'

'Or perhaps,' Faith said suddenly, 'it was supposed to look like the writing on the suitcase. Let's find out who left the note.' She went to reception.

The man in the bow tie was courteous but apologetic. The note had been on the desk by the telephone when he came on duty, and he had just followed its instructions. He had no idea where it came from.

'Well, that was absolutely no help,' Faith said. 'Mystery on mystery. I think it must have been Laval, though I can't see what he stood to gain from it.'

'What did he want, anyway?' Hannibal said.

In her concern over the note, Faith had completely forgotten about the car, but when she led the way to the door, there, parked beside the pavement, in the shade of an oleander, was the little blue hatchback. She went over to it, and peered through the window. There was a map, as Laval had promised. And there was something else. In the window a little sticker . . . Johnnie's Car Hire.

'Car hire,' she said, aloud. 'I thought from what he said that it was a private car. Perhaps that is why he could afford to be so generous. Or is Mr Laval such a very big wheel that the car company will let him have it for nothing?'

Hannibal laughed, a dry, mocking laugh. 'Oh, he's a bigger wheel than that. Mr Laval is the hire car company. He owns it.'

5

If Laval owned the car-hire company, then he was the one indirectly responsible for leaving her stranded at the airport, Faith thought to herself. Always assuming that it was the same hire company, but yes, she was sure that she had seen the name Johnnie's Hire on invoices in London. Somehow, that realisation made her feel more comfortable.

'Well,' she said to Hannibal, 'if this is the car I should have had in the first place, I shan't mind using it.'

She expected him to laugh with her, but he looked uncomfortable, and cast a worried glance towards the hotel.

'What is it?' she wanted to know.

He smiled. 'Oh, nothing, just that there will no doubt be trouble for some poor soul because your car wasn't where you expected it.'

'I should think so, too,' Faith retorted. 'It was extremely inconvenient.'

Hannibal looked grave. 'Yes, but Laval can be particularly vindictive when he chooses. And it's not always the guilty who suffer.'

'What do you mean by that? Are you suggesting that I'm guilty?'

He managed a smile. 'Of course not. I just don't trust Laval. When things go wrong around him, somebody always seem to be in serious trouble.'

'There was serious trouble for somebody this time, all right,' Faith said, in an attempt to cheer him up. 'I had to drive back from the airport with you.'

This time Hannibal did laugh. 'Yes, indeed,' he said, 'and even then you might be more right than you know!'

'I wish you would stop talking in riddles,' Faith said, seriously.

He smiled, that deep, warm, secret smile that lit his whole face.

'I think it's time I stopped talking altogether,' he said, 'and took you to see

Valetta, since that is what I promised.' He grinned towards the hatchback. 'Your car or mine?'

'Let's use Laval's petrol,' Faith said. 'He said he'd left a tankful, and I've only got today and tomorrow — my plane leaves first thing on Thursday.'

She had meant it to be a light-hearted comment, but the words left her with a lump in her throat. It seemed like no time at all.

Hannibal said nothing, but took the key from her hand and opened the driver's door. Faith was ready to fume inwardly — just like Charles, assuming that if there was any driving to be done, he was the one to do it, although he was obviously twice the driver that Charles was.

But she had misjudged him. Hannibal was standing with the door open, for her to get in.

'No, you drive,' she said, and then realised that he had been waiting for her to say just that. All the same, he had not automatically assumed the right, and she was grateful for that.

The road wound down beside a deep, wide basin, where a host of small, sailing boats bobbed at anchor. Across the bay, a host of white cruising yachts lifted their masts into the midday sunshine, and their reflections sparkled in the blue water.

But then the car turned up steeply, past a bus station and a little park. Hannibal drew the car to a halt in a shady corner and switched off the engine.

Faith got out of the car, and he led the way past stalls selling every imaginable thing. They turned a corner and there before them loomed the arched entrance to the city.

'Down here,' Hannibal directed, taking her elbow and steering her down a narrow street. It was crowded, so crowded that it seemed she was looking at a river — made up of sunshades, shirts, dresses, printed scarves — each colour moving against the rest in a tireless pattern of kaleidoscope. She stood still to watch, and heard the camera click and whirr.

'You took a photograph?'

He smiled, and handed her the camera. 'You looked so pretty. It will give you something to remember this morning by.'

'I shan't need to be reminded,' she said, softly. 'I'll never forget it.'

Certainly, it was memorable. The streets were so steep that they were built as a series of shallow steps. A new church stood at every other street corner. Bunches of electric wire, looped from house to house, and entered the buildings through little, rough holes in the wall.

'A drink first, I think,' Hannibal said, leading the way into a large open square where a series of gay umbrellas filled the wide pavement. 'And then lunch.'

'There are some beautiful things here,' Faith said, looking into his smiling, dark eyes.

They had eaten a well-prepared meal

of beef olives washed down with mineral water. Hannibal raised his glass of water in a mock toast.

'Especially today.'

Faith felt herself colour like a schoolgirl.

Later, as they were sipping coffee, Hannibal glanced at his watch. 'It's time for you to have a look around. There is one place, though, that I would like to take you — to the war museum.'

'The war museum?' She was puzzled. She knew that Malta had received the George Cross for heroism during the Second World War, and Hannibal's conversation had shown her how very significant the bombardment of the island had been, but all the same, it seemed an odd place for a rendezvous.

He smiled. 'I want you to meet Faith,' he said.

Her heart lurched. 'Who's Faith?'

His smile broadened. 'She's an aeroplane,' he said, and laughed aloud at her obvious astonishment. 'No, really — though she is an old lady now. At the beginning of the war there were only three planes available to defend the island against the entire Italian air-force — three little bi-planes, and they were in crates, and had to be assembled before they could fly. Little Gloster Gladiators, but they were plucky, little planes, and some very plucky, young men flew them. Later on, there were other planes of course — Spitfires and Hurricanes among them — but it was those three that caught the imagination. Faith, Hope and Charity, people called them. And now only Faith is left — in the War Museum.'

'That's an amazing story,' Faith breathed.

'This is an amazing island,' he returned. 'But now, really, I must go. I'll leave you this plan of the city. I'll see you here again in what — an hour and a half?'

She gaped at him. 'You're going?'

He made a little face. 'Work, I'm afraid. An American client and his wife, here on a flying visit about this new leisure complex we are building. I shouldn't be too long. I've got a programme arranged for them this afternoon and it doesn't require me. He's going to talk to our financial director, and I've arranged for her to have a fashion show, so all I have to do is to pick them up from the airport, give them a chance to wash and brush up, and then take them to their next appointments. I'll be back by four.'

'Is that all right?' Faith said. 'It doesn't sound very professional.'

'My job is to keep the punters happy,' Hannibal said. 'I don't have to be there personally. And they're only planning to be here for a few hours.'

'Punters?' Faith found the word distasteful, and her voice showed it.

'Well, visitors then,' Hannibal said. 'A fellow's got to make a living.'

But he was still looking uncomfortable as he paid the waiter and the colourful sea of passers-by swallowed him up.

* * *

The crowded city seemed somehow empty without him, and for ten minutes or so Faith simply drifted, allowing the tide of shoppers to carry her along. Then she stopped to take stock. She had so little time in Malta and it would be sensible to use it more wisely.

There was such a lot to do that it was hard to decide, but at last she opted for the cathedral and a visit to the film show about Malta in wartime.

The cathedral was beautiful, cool and dignified with gilded pictures on every wall. Even on a Tuesday afternoon the church was full, not only of sightseers, though there were plenty of them, but also of local men and women kneeling in the chapels where the candles glowed.

A man in a red shirt, who had slipped into the church behind her, edged into a pew and bent over his rosary.

Faith was not religious herself, but

the simplicity of their devotion moved her. It was fitting, she felt, that the little aeroplane to survive on this island was the one called Faith. She came out again on to the street and the heat hit her like a hammer.

She reached the film show just as a showing was about to begin. Some of the scenes shocked her — the statue of Queen Victoria which she had so recently seen sitting serenely in the peaceful square, pictured here incongruously enthroned amidst a scene of total desolation, in which every building around was reduced to rubble. And there, photographed in flight, the little bi-planes Hannibal had spoken of. Which one of them was Faith, she wondered idly.

The daylight seemed particularly bright afterwards, and as she emerged out into it, she stood for a moment blinking in the sun. A man, crossing the road close by her, glanced towards her for a moment and, meeting her eyes, looked away again and hurried on.

Faith felt a faint clenching of her stomach.

It was the man in the red shirt.

Faith fought down her panic and went to sit under the umbrellas. Here, in public view, she could come to no harm.

She ordered an ice-cream. They brought her a symphony in a bowl, and she might have enjoyed the extravagance had she not seen, from the corner of her eye, a man in a red shirt settle at a table at the far end of the café and bury his head in a newspaper.

Odd that she had not been conscious before that someone was following her, but until she had glimpsed his face, she had not really registered the man's presence. Where was it she had seen him before?

She sat up so suddenly that she knocked the spoon from the glass of ice-cream. The security man at Laval's office! That was where she'd seen him, she was absolutely certain of it. She turned back to check her recollection, but the man, perhaps aware of her scrutiny, folded his paper and moved off, whistling. She was still staring after him when Hannibal appeared.

'Am I glad to see you!' she said, as he slid down into the chair opposite.

'And I'm glad to see you,' he returned, and then, seeing her face, added more seriously, 'What's the matter?'

'You may think I'm stupid,' she said, 'but this is beginning to get me down. I think there is someone following me.' She explained her suspicions. 'Perhaps I am imagining things,' she finished, lamely, 'but what with that note this morning, and now this ... I'm beginning to feel very uneasy. And I'm sure that man is one of Laval's employees. I just wish I could be as sure of where I've seen that maid at the hotel before.'

Hannibal was looking at her intently, a faint flush showing under the brown skin. 'The maid?' he said sharply.

'You've seen her before? You can't have done.'

'I can't place it,' Faith said meditatively, 'but there is something about that face that I recognise. Anyway,' she went on, 'I'm sure I recognise that man!'

'Where is he?' Hannibal said. 'Can you see him now?'

She glanced around. 'No,' she said. 'He disappeared a few moments before you arrived.'

He made a little face. 'Damn Laval! Spoiling an otherwise near-perfect afternoon.'

'You think it was Laval who put him up to it?'

Hannibal nodded. 'Who else could it be? No-one else knows you.'

'It could be chance, I suppose.'

'Do you believe that?' And then, as she shook her head, 'Neither do I. So it must be Laval.'

'I don't know how Laval knew where we were going today. Perhaps I said something. I don't altogether remember,' she said doubtfully.

He threw his head back and laughed. 'That's not like you. When I picked you up from the airport you seemed to file away every word I said and use it in evidence against me! I was beginning to think you mentally tape-recorded every conversation!'

'Well, you did seem to know a lot about me,' she said, and the smile died on her lips as the doubts and uncertainties of the day before returned. 'Hannibal, tell me the truth, do you know Stephanie Ranier?'

His eyes met hers, steady and brown. 'I promise you Faith, I've never met anyone of that name in all my life.'

She believed him. He was so open, so sincere, she could not doubt him. But she said, hesitantly, 'So why did you go to the airport? Was it really just an accident that you met me? And how did you know where I was staying?'

The eyes faltered and fell. 'It's a long story.'

'Tell me.'

He glanced around nervously. 'Yes,' he said at last, 'I think perhaps I will. But not here. Too many walls have ears. Look, my Americans will be on the plane by seven. Why don't I take you back to the hotel, and you can freshen up and change, and I'll come back and take you out to dinner somewhere. We could go over to the east side of the island. There are some old fishing villages there, with all the traditional fishing boats in the harbour, and if you like swordfish — '

She laughed. 'Not every night!'

'There is more than one fish in the sea. Isn't that what you English say?'

She laughed again. 'Yes, but we don't usually mean it so literally.' Soon, she thought sadly, she would have to console herself with that thought. In less than forty-eight hours she would be back in London. How dreary the grey streets would seem after this Mediterranean paradise. And Charles. How pompous and dreary he would seem.

'I'll have to try a new fish,' she said, half to herself.

'Then you will come?'

'I'd love to — ' Faith began, and then recollection stopped her. 'Oh, no! Of course, I can't. I promised Charles I would be in the hotel this evening, so that he could get in touch. Between seven and nine, we said. I thought I'd be certain to be there for dinner.' She had been grateful, at the time, for Charles's suggestion, imagining long, lonely evenings in an unfamiliar hotel.

Hannibal was looking at her intently. 'Charles?'

'Someone I know in London,' she said lightly. 'He likes to keep an eye on me, make sure I'm safe.'

'Safe from whom?' Hannibal said gently.

She met his eyes and kept her voice teasing. 'Well, from handsome and charming, young, Maltese gentlemen, among others.'

But he would not be deflected. His hand closed over hers. 'And are you?

85

Safe from them?'

Something in his tone made her catch her breath, and she said quietly, 'Not altogether.'

He moved closer, his lips almost brushing her hair. 'I'm glad.'

Her heart was pounding but she said, 'You don't want me to be safe?'

'Safe with me, not safe from me,' Hannibal said, and he looked deep into her eyes for a long, lingering moment.

'Coffee, sir?' The waiter's voice interrupted them, and Faith sprang back, embarrassed. She had half-forgotten they were in a public place.

'Just the bill, I think,' Hannibal said, and then as the waiter hurried away, 'And you cannot disappoint him, this Charles from London?'

Faith smiled ruefully. 'You don't know Charles. If I wasn't there when he rang, he'd be on the next plane looking for me. He's quite convinced I couldn't find my way across the street without him to guide me, so if I don't answer his call, he'll suspect white slave traffic at the very least.'

Hannibal did not smile. 'He must value you a great deal.'

She said, wryly, 'Charles values all his possessions. His mistake is in thinking I'm one of them.' She frowned as she realised the truth in her words. She would never be anything more than a treasured possession to Charles. Aloud she said, 'He doesn't own me. He's asked me to marry him a dozen times, and I've always refused. He has no rights over me at all. He just thinks he has.'

Somehow, just voicing those words gave her a feeling of freedom and release. She smiled at Hannibal. 'So you see, he is just an ex-boyfriend. But he does worry about me, so I will stay and take his call, because I said I would.'

Hannibal was smiling back. 'But if I came later, and called for you, you wouldn't object?'

She smiled again, a firm confident

smile. 'I should love it.'

Hannibal got to his feet. 'Then the sooner the better!' The movement brought the waiter scampering over with the bill. Hannibal paid it, and took her arm as they left the café and strolled companionably back to the car.

'You drive then,' she said, and they drove back to the hotel in contented silence.

Hannibal drew up under the shade of the wall, and handed her the keys.

'After dinner then.'

'After dinner.' She gave him a quick smile, and he gave her arm a squeeze, but all the same it was painful to leave him, even for a few hours. Perhaps she could see him from the balcony.

She hurried into her room and threw open the window. Hannibal was still on the street, opening the door of the coupé. As she watched, he nodded his head in salute, not to her, for he had not glanced in her direction, but to somebody in the street. She craned a little farther forward, to see better.

Emerging from a car on the corner was a man in a red shirt . . .

6

No, she had not imagined it. She had seen it with her own eyes. The man had looked at Hannibal and something had passed between them. A signal? Recognition? She sat down on the bed, her thoughts racing.

Hannibal! Was it possible that he had set the man to follow her? After all, Red Shirt had appeared shortly after Hannibal had left her, and, she realised with a little shudder, he had disappeared again only a moment or two before Hannibal himself came back. And who but Hannibal knew that she was in Valetta?

But why would he do that? Why for that matter, had he collected her at the airport? There were so many unanswered questions.

A long story, he had said. Well, she would give him the benefit of the doubt, at least until she had heard his explanations. Perhaps tonight he would set her mind at rest. In the meantime, she would shower, change and perhaps take a moment or two to Fax her report to Brenda. It would be cheaper to do that now, after office hours, and since she was not bringing home a lucrative contract she could at least practise these little economies.

Suddenly, she remembered the night before, when someone had searched her luggage, and on an impulse she went over to the desk and peered inside. Yes, the report was there, lying safely on the sales folder where she had left it that morning. Take a grip of yourself, Faith, she told herself severely. You are getting paranoid. Who on earth would want to tamper with your silly sales report?

She went into the bathroom and began to run the shower, humming to herself. She was about to slip her dress over her head and abandon herself to cool, clear water when a realisation froze her in her tracks.

Slowly, like one in a dream, she

turned off the taps and went back into the bedroom. Her hands were trembling as she pulled open the drawer.

Yes, her eyes did not deceive her. The report was there on top of the sales folder, but she had left it inside the folder. She was certain of that. She had made a point of slipping the report inside the folder and putting the whole thing into the drawer.

Quickly, she turned over the pages. It was all there. Nothing was missing. Nothing had been added, or subtracted. Nothing had been changed. Only, someone had come to her room, taken the folder and looked at the report. Read it, more than likely. The evidence was undeniable.

It could not be Hannibal. That was her first thought. Hannibal had been with her in Valetta. And then, hard on the heels of that thought, came the sober realisation — no, he had left her and gone to see his punters, or so he claimed. In that time he could easily have driven to the hotel and come into her room. After all, he knew the number, he had delivered her luggage here yesterday.

But what for? What could he possibly hope to gain? Or anybody else for that matter? There was nothing in those papers but a factual account of her interview with Laval. It didn't make sense.

Well, she had had enough. First her luggage had been searched, and now this. Whatever else, hotel security should have prevented it.

She went to the room telephone and dialled zero. The young man from reception answered it, she recognised the voice.

'Will you put me through to the management, please,' Faith said, surprised how calm her voice sounded. 'I want to make a complaint.'

Somehow, voicing her problems publicly, Faith felt better. The deputy manager, a tall Scot with a quiet manner, came to her room and listened to her politely.

'I'm terribly sorry, Miss Worthing. I don't know how such a thing could possibly have happened. We've never had the slightest problems before. You are quite sure, are you, that you haven't made a mistake?'

'Quite sure!' Faith snapped. Did the man take her for an idiot?

'But nothing is missing?' the deputy manager persisted.

'No, fortunately.' It was obvious what he was driving at, and Faith allowed her irritation to show. 'Otherwise I should have called the police. I am rather tempted to do so anyway.'

That changed his tune. He said, in a placatory voice, 'There is so very little crime on Malta — but I suppose in a hotel, there is always the possibility . . . The best I can do, Miss Worthing, is to offer you another room, opposite the housekeeper's office. There is always someone on duty there, and I can promise you that no-one would be able to enter your room unobserved. Fortunately we have a number of vacancies this week, so there should be no problem at all in managing that.'

It was such a practical proposal that Faith felt a little foolish, as if the wind had been taken out of her sails, and she said crossly, 'It should never have happened in the first place. The room was locked — it can only have been someone with a key.'

The deputy manager looked shocked. 'I can't imagine it was one of our staff, Miss Worthing, unless it was just plain nosiness, but I find that very hard to believe. We've never had a complaint of this nature before.'

'Then what are you suggesting?' she said sharply. 'That someone else came in and asked for my room key? Would the staff have given it to them then?'

The deputy manager looked doubtful. 'I don't think so. Of course, it is a fairly large hotel and the reception staff don't always remember which guest is in which room. But an intruder would have to get the key from reception and return it, and the staff would certainly not part with the key to anyone they did not know. No, I should have thought it very unlikely. But I'll look into it, I promise you. I'll ask all the housekeeping staff. Perhaps one of them saw something.'

'Ask that little maid with the towels,' Faith said, suddenly seeing a vision of the girl scuttling away like a frightened rabbit. Was she in the habit of searching the rooms for valuables? 'I wonder . . . ?'

'Yes?' the deputy manager said sharply.

'Oh, nothing,' Faith said. 'It was just a thought.' If it had been the maid, she looked haunted enough. The fact that the management was making enquiries would teach her never to do it again, and after all, nothing was missing. That poor girl looked terrified already, without Faith voicing her suspicions.

'We'll find you a new room as soon as we can,' the manager said. 'I'll tell the housekeeper to get it ready — we've had a group cancel this week, so I know that one will be available. In the meantime, if you are going to have dinner in the hotel, please accept a bottle of wine with your meal, with our compliments.'

'Thank you,' Faith said.

The practical, down-to-earth discussion had made her feel better, and she showered and went down to dinner in a much more tranquil state of mind.

It might, perhaps, have been that complimentary bottle of wine which gave her the courage, but on the way back up to her room she stopped on an impulse and rang the bell at reception. 'We'll look into it,' the deputy manager had said. Well, she would look into it a little herself.

The man with the bow tie came out of the office. *Keith, Senior Receptionist*, it said on his badge. 'Can I help you?' And then, as he recognised her. 'Did you manage to sort out your problems?'

'Yes, thank you,' Faith said. 'There is

just one thing. Have you been on duty all afternoon?'

'Since two o'clock.'

Faith made a mental calculation. At two o'clock she had been with Hannibal in Valetta. 'And have there been any callers for me? Anyone asking for my key?'

He shook his head. 'Not that I'm aware of. Of course, I have to leave the desk from time to time, but I'm sure I'd have seen anyone. Were you expecting anyone in particular?'

'I wondered whether Mr Price — Hannibal — might have come here looking for me. The gentleman who brought my bags in yesterday. Do you know him?'

Keith flushed painfully. 'Well, I've seen him now, of course, but he was here before my time. I've only been here a month or two. Mind you,' he said, conspiratorially, dropping his voice to a whisper, 'I know a lot of the staff think the whole thing was blown out of all proportion, and that there must have been a reasonable explanation for it.'

Faith stared at him. 'For what? What are you talking about?'

The young man gazed at her in alarm. 'I'm sorry, Miss Worthing, I've spoken out of turn. I shouldn't have said anything.'

'Said anything about what?' Faith repeated, and then, working it out in her mind. 'What do you mean before your time? Are you telling me that Hannibal Price worked at this hotel?'

'Well,' Keith said unhappily. 'I suppose you'll find out sooner or later. Yes, he did. He was deputy manager here.'

'And he was dismissed?' Faith guessed, putting two and two together.

'Yes. Though a lot of the staff think it was a put-up job, as I say. He was found in the manager's office apparently, in the middle of the night, going through the owner's private papers. Dismissed him on the spot.'

'The owner?' Faith said, but she already knew the answer.

'Yes,' Keith said. 'Mr Laval.'

Faith want back to her room in a daze. So that was it! Hannibal had been dismissed for dishonesty. No wonder he disliked Laval so intensely. No wonder, for that matter, that Laval had warned her against Hannibal.

Was it possible? Was Hannibal the kind of man who would search through private papers? Her own things had been searched, not once, but twice. Yes, she had to admit, it was only too possible.

It would make sense, too. After all, she had come to do business with Laval, had been to a meeting with him. Anyone who wanted to spy into his business could do a lot worse than waylay Faith Worthing at the airport, separate her from her luggage, and have a quick search through it. To say nothing of the report she would obviously write afterwards. For anyone who had ever had access to the keys of the hotel it was easy.

Particularly easy, she thought with a sudden chill, for anyone who was familiar with the hotel booking system. As the ex-deputy manager, Hannibal might well have known that she was coming. A quick telephone call to cancel the hire car, a run out to the airport to meet a contact who conveniently failed to arrive, and it was an easy business to give a certain Miss Worthing a lift back to Sleima, and her appointment with Laval.

And what about Stephanie Rainier? If Hannibal Price had once been the deputy manager of the hotel, then of course he knew Stephanie. She had been there several times. Unwelcome as it was, it seemed that Laval had been right.

She shook her head. She could not, would not, believe it. Hannibal had promised her an explanation. Until she had heard him out, she would try to give him the benefit of the doubt. But what kind of doubt could there be, she asked herself miserably, when the damning information came from a young man who, by his own admission, had never clapped eyes on Hannibal until yesterday.

The sound of the telephone made her start. She picked up the receiver with trembling hands.

'Miss Worthing? A call for you.'

She could feel her throat constrict as she waited. She wanted, more than anything else, for Hannibal to tell her that everything was all right, that her suspicions were groundless, that there was a rational explanation for all this. She only wished she could think of one for herself. And yet she must be careful. If he did want to meet her to give an explanation, it had better be in some public place, like the bar. The eyes of the terrified, little maid still haunted her.

'Fay, my dear girl, how are you coping?'

Relief and disappointment flooded over her in equal measure.

'Charles! Is that you?'

'Of course it's me. Don't be such a little silly-billy. Who else would it be?' Charles admonished. 'I wanted to check up on your arrival arrangements. You go and get your ticket and read me the flight details.'

For a moment the impulse to confess her problems overcame her. 'Charles,' she began, 'there's something I wanted to talk to you about — '

'First things first, Fay,' Charles said heartily. 'You go and get that ticket, like a good girl.'

She obeyed, and he read back the flight number and arrival time to double check them.

'Now, I'll be at the airport so there is nothing for you to worry about. Four o'clock Thursday. And you won't forget the time difference, will you?'

'Charles, I've been in Malta for two days. Of course I've changed my watch.'

'Well, you can't be too careful,' he said. 'How did the meeting go, anyway?'

'I didn't get the contract.'

There was a slight pause, and then he

said, 'No? Oh, well, never mind. I didn't really think you would. Still, don't worry. I'm sure Stephanie and Brenda will sort it out. Now, listen, write this down so you don't forget it. Make sure you've got your ticket and your passport in your handbag when you get to the airport. Don't go leaving them in your briefcase, or you'll have to put your handbag down while you look for them, and you know what airports are like.'

'Yes, Charles,' she said meekly.

'There's a good girl,' he said. 'Now, what did you want to ask me about?'

'Oh,' she said, 'nothing much. I'll see you Thursday.'

'I'm looking forward to it,' Charles's voice was hearty. 'And we'll go out for a nice lobster supper afterwards, shall we? You take care now.' And he was gone.

Faith put down the telephone slowly. She should have told him about Hannibal. Charles would have known what to do. And he would have loved telling her so.

She stood for a moment, almost ready to pick up the telephone and ring him back, and then she straightened resolutely. No, darn it, she would not go grovelling to Charles. He would only treat her as if she was a three-year-old, and an idiot three-year-old at that. She would stand on her own two feet. And the first thing she would do was ask a few questions of Hannibal Price.

She glanced at her watch. It was a moment or two after nine. Just time, she thought to herself, to send that Fax to Brenda. Then, when Hannibal came, she would hear what he had to say, and make up her own mind.

She picked up the report and made her way downstairs.

'I believe I can Fax from here,' she said. 'You can put it on the bill. It's company business.'

'Just along to the right,' the young man said. 'And there is a message for you.' He handed her a slip of folded paper.

She opened it. *Telephone message*

from Mr H. Price. He will be unable to meet you this evening. Something urgent has cropped up. He will be in touch tomorrow.

He wasn't coming! Disappointment hit her like a physical blow. The Americans must have decided to stay a little longer. Unless this was another of Laval's games. She sent her Fax, and then went back into the foyer and waited.

Hannibal did not come. It was hard to believe how much she wanted to see him again, wanted to believe in him. She looked up. The receptionist was looking at her anxiously. 'Is everything all right?'

'Fine,' she said, hurriedly, although she was very far from feeling it. She went out into the warm, heavy, evening air.

It was dark, but although it was late, the tourist shops were open, and she spent a little while wandering among them. Then, unwilling to go back to the hotel, she sat in a café with a cup of coffee, watching the crowds go by.

Everyone seemed to be in pairs, and when at last she paid her bill and got up to go, she was very aware of being alone. The streets, though thronged with people, seemed alien and threatening, and she hurried along, anxious for the familiar security of the hotel.

There were couples everywhere. On one dark corner, Faith actually collided with a pair of dark shapes. They glanced up, startled at the impact, and Faith glimpsed their faces — his urgent and concerned, hers tear-strained and trusting — before the young man drew the girl back into the shadows and they moved away.

Faith muttered an apology and hurried on, embarrassed, but she had not gone half a dozen paces before realisation hit her, and she stopped, transfixed.

She whirled around, but the young couple had vanished into the night. Faith turned back slowly, and made her way up the steps of the hotel, her feelings of isolation sickening to despair.

She had no right to feel this way. But as she tossed sleeplessly, those faces haunted her mind — Hannibal Price, and in his arms, the little hotel maid.

7

Morning brought no relief. It was hopeless, simply hopeless, and the sooner she realised the fact the better. Hannibal Price was a womaniser, a cheat and a liar. He had abandoned her for something urgent — and she knew now what that was.

'Bit of cloud this morning,' the breakfast waitress said, 'but it'll soon go.'

And so shall I, Faith thought, and the realisation seemed almost welcome.

She was almost glad, on her way up from the dining-room, to find Laval in the foyer. He seemed to be waiting for her.

He came over, smiling. 'You found the car satisfactory?'

She forced her warmest smile in return. 'Very satisfactory, thank you.'

'You enjoyed Valetta?'

'How did you know I had been there?'

He laughed. 'Young Fabio, my security guard, mentioned that he'd seen you. 'Keeping an eye on you,' he said. Following a pretty girl around, I call it! He's always had a weak spot for blondes, and you've made a conquest there. I hope he didn't make a nuisance of himself. You probably saw him, knowing Fabio.'

So that explained Red Shirt. And she had been half-ready to accuse Laval of having her followed. Or Hannibal, for that matter. Some of the tension drained out of her. 'Yes,' she said, 'as a matter of fact I did see him. I wondered what was going on.'

Laval smiled. 'He said you seemed a bit alarmed. I'm sorry about that. I'll have a word with him about it. Though I can hardly blame him. You are pretty.'

She made a little grimace. 'No, please don't concern yourself. It's just, this last couple of days, everything has been so unsettling. I suppose I was ready to see conspiracy everywhere.'

It was Hannibal's fault, she reflected bitterly. He had managed to persuade her to regard a bit of teenage infatuation as a sinister threat. Poor Fabio. He had hardly been pestering her.

And if that was Laval's security guard, it explained why there was recognition between him and Hannibal on the street. As an ex-employee, Hannibal would know the security man.

She said aloud, 'I've been letting my fancy run away with me. I expect it is being abroad for the first time.'

Laval looked sympathetic. 'And now I hear you have had an unfortunate experience with your papers, too. It is not surprising you are feeling a little bit on edge. I've had a few enquiries made, and I think I know who was responsible. The person concerned has been dismissed, of course. It is lucky that you were so alert and we've been able to stamp it out before anything actually went missing. It could have happened to any of our guests.'

But Faith was following her own train of thought. 'No,' she said, 'it would only have happened to me.'

The smile died on Laval's lip. 'What do you mean?' His voice was sharp.

Faith said slowly, 'It was that little maid, wasn't it?' It was all fitting into place. Hannibal had come to the hotel, asking for Miss Worthing's room number. He had even brought the luggage. No wonder the poor kid — who was presumably his girl-friend — had been so curious. What had she been looking for? Love letters? Faith sighed. 'I think I know what this was all about.'

Laval was looking at her intently. 'What do you mean?' he asked again.

'Jealousy,' Faith said, ruefully.

'Jealousy?' Laval sounded incredulous.

'I saw that girl with Hannibal last night,' she said, softly. 'I think those two may have a . . . well, a relationship.'

'I see.' Laval shot her a glance. 'You may well be right.' There was a little pause, and then he went on, 'Have you spoken to Mr Price since?'

She shook her head. 'No. He was supposed to call for me last night, but I had a message to say that he was unavoidably called away. And now I know where. He was going to get in touch this morning, but I'm beginning to decide that I won't bother to wait for his call.' She gave Laval a faint smile. 'I'm inclined to believe that I've let myself be beguiled by a pair of big, brown eyes.'

Laval patted her shoulder, gently. 'I did warn you.'

'I know. But I wasn't sure that I could trust you, either. I didn't realise that he had actually worked for you, and that you had solid ground for your distrust.'

'Who told you that?' Laval said, his voice suddenly cold.

'The young man at reception,' Faith said. 'I was asking him about Hannibal.'

Laval said sharply. 'What did he say?'

'Not a lot,' Faith said. 'Only that Hannibal was dismissed for going through your private papers. I don't think he knew any more than that. He didn't even recognise Hannibal the first time he saw him. Anyway,' she went on, giving him a warm smile, 'it's just as well he did tell me. At least, hearing it from an outsider, I now know whom to trust.'

Laval's face cleared. 'I suppose you are right,' he said, reluctantly. 'Perhaps you should avoid hospitality managers in the future. It might have been Price, you know, who searched your case.'

'Whatever for?'

'Money?' and then as she shook her head, 'Documents perhaps. Look at the way he went through mine! He may even have hoped to pick up Moonlight Cosmetics as a client for that leisure company of his. They do promotional hospitality for big internationals. Who knows?'

Faith shrugged. 'I suppose in the long

run there is no harm done. The trouble is, I feel so — I don't know — exploited, somehow. I'll just have to make sure I don't run into him again.'

Laval nodded. 'I think that would be very wise. Why don't you take the car and go somewhere for the day? You could take a trip to Gozo. You'd hardly be likely to run into him there. I have contacts there who would be happy to show you around.'

She shook her head. 'I haven't enough money,' she said. 'The ferry costs money, and I didn't come prepared for holidaymaking.'

Laval smiled. 'That's easily remedied. Here.' He took out his wallet and handed her a small, printed pass. 'I have business interests in Gozo, and I have a lot of traffic going to and fro. This is a pre-paid pass for the ferry. No, you catch the morning ferry and go to this address.' He handed her a printed card. 'I will ring my friend who runs a small restaurant in Rabat — Victoria as you probably know it — I'd be delighted to pick up your bill for lunch, and get one of my staff to meet you and take you to see the rest of the island. It is the least I can do after all your problems with my hire-car firm and my hotel.'

'And your importing business,' she said on an impulse.

Laval shot her a look. 'Meaning?'

'That I didn't manage to take home that contract.'

Laval laughed. 'Trying a little moral blackmail to see if I'll change my mind? I tell you what — you tell Stephanie to come over as soon as ever she is well enough, and I'll be ready to sign the biggest contract ever. Will that do?'

It was certainly better than nothing. Brenda would be pleased, after all. Faith was even smiling a little as she helped the porter to move her suitcases to a new, larger room. Then she went down to the car and set off for the ferry port. At least she could have an entertaining day in Gozo.

* * *

She had a moment of guilt as she edged the little, blue hatchback out into the traffic, and glimpsed, in her rear-view mirror, a black coupé drawing up at the hotel entrance. But she hardened her heart and drove grimly out through the narrow streets. Hannibal Price deserved nothing from her.

It was the first time she had driven in Malta, and she tried to concentrate on the experience, and not think about anything else.

She reached the ferry and squeezed on to the car-deck. She had picked up a booklet at the hotel and was already making plans about what she wanted to see. The prehistoric temples, Calypso's cave, a quick look at the walled city and the church of the miracles and it would be time to catch the ferry home.

Gozo had looked a mere stone's throw away across the water, but it took more than half-an-hour, and she was impatient until they arrived, and she could drive away on to the island.

She found the restaurant without difficulty. The owner, a puffing, fat man in a crumpled suit, appointed himself as guide and announced that there was just time to see the temples before lunch. They were amazing — mighty, ancient structures — older than the Pyramids, he told her — with their grotesque goddesses and massive, stone altars. It was an enchanted place, and she tried to forget Hannibal Price, and her wounded pride, by drinking in the mighty pillars and the purple-pink of the bougainvillaea.

But her guide was impatient. The ancient site meant little to him, and though he was obsequious in his desire to please, he was clearly anxious to return to his restaurant before midday. She allowed herself to be persuaded, and although she was not hungry, ordered a simple spaghetti and a glass of local wine, to his obvious disappointment. He spent several minutes trying to persuade her to more exotic fare.

After lunch, though, she could not face subjecting herself to an afternoon of the restaurateur's oily company, and she excused herself, declaring her intention to browse the market stalls. But after half-an-hour she abandoned her window-shopping. Her heart was not in it, and her limited budget would not stretch to such indulgences. Casting a guilty look in the direction of the restaurant, she made her way back to the car, and glad of her own company, followed the signposts towards Calypso's Cave.

It was a tortuous narrow, winding road, and, more than once, she wondered if she had taken the wrong turning. The signposts were not easy to see, and when she reached a remote crossroads where roadworks were in progress, she realised that she had lost her sense of direction altogether. Had there been a driver in the road-digger at the roadside, she would have asked him, but the man had evidently gone away for his lunch. She looked around for guidance, and finding none, decided to try to find her way back to the main road by turning down a narrow, dusty lane which forked away to her left. It went towards the sea, she reasoned, and that was where the tourists went.

It was the wrong way. That much was obvious in less than half-a-mile. The road led to a house, set back in garden ablaze with geraniums, and decorative thistles of a startling blue, but beyond that it degenerated into little more than a rocky track, set between dusty-gold, stone walls.

She thought about trying to turn around, but there was not enough space between the walls, and she drove on slowly. The track was evidently used, and she was heartened to see an old notice nailed to a rotting post. Somebody had painted over the wording, as though it were out-of-date, but it was possible to make it out, all the same. **Fireworks Factory. Keep out.**

Faith had heard about the fireworks, used at the religious ceremonies throughout the islands, and apparently very spectacular, but this factory had clearly ceased production. There was, though, likely to be at least an entrance where she might reasonably find enough space to turn the car. A moment later, as she turned a corner, she saw the compound — a huddle of old sheds and stone buildings behind a tall fence. She drove forward with renewed confidence.

To her horror, however, Faith saw, beyond the nearer wall, a pall of white dust beginning to rise. It grew gradually nearer, creeping up the hill along the line of the wall, and she realised that it was caused by a vehicle. Something was driving up the track towards her.

It was a problem she had not even considered, but there was nothing for it. She would have to inch her painful way backwards to the gateway of the house she had seen at the top of the road in order to let the vehicle pass.

The oncoming vehicle was heavy, from the sound of it, and from the speed it was making. It would be a tight squeeze, but at least it gave her some time. Slamming the car into reverse, she began the nerve-racking business of inching back up the twisting road, towards the house. She just had time to reach the safety of the gateway, and tuck the car into the entranceway, before the van lumbered past her with barely an inch to spare.

Faith frowned, as she read the words painted on the side of the van in six-inch letters. **Laval Enterprises. Gozo.**

Well, what was so odd about that? There was no need to feel that little tingle of fear. Mr Laval had said he had business interests in Gozo. This, presumably, was one of them. It was a strange, out-of-the-way place, certainly, but if there was a disused factory going begging, it obviously made sense to use it, even in Gozo. There was nothing to be suspicious about.

Faith considered her predicament and decided that her best option was to carry on down the track until she found a suitable place to turn the car. Mr Laval would have no objection to her having a little look at his factory, since she accidentally stumbled upon it. He could hardly object to her trying to avoid scratching his car's paintwork!

She let out the clutch and edged forward again. The air was still thick with the dust which the van had raised, but she drove resolutely through it, hoping that no more vans were lurching towards her in this dusty fog. Nothing came, and she drove without incident all the way to a wide entrance with huge, steel gates. The gates were padlocked, and the notice on them was new, and decidedly unfriendly. **Private Packaging Plant. Keep Out.**

Several vans were parked in the enclosure, all bearing the Laval logo. There were half a dozen overflowing dustbins, and, in an open-sided shed, Faith could see crate upon crate of cardboard boxes and wooden packing cases. A pile of discarded cardboard, yellowing and curling in the sun, lay against one of the walls. Otherwise, the enclosure appeared to be empty.

She swung the car around as best she could, but although the gateway was wide, the gates themselves filled the entrance, and there was very little more room that there had been outside the house. She made three attempts to manoeuvre the little hatchback, but it was obvious that this was going to be a long, slow business.

Scowling, she got out and rattled the gates. Presumably the driver of the van had been the last person on the premises, and he had gone to lunch, but there was always a chance that there was someone inside. She walked along the fence, hoping to see some sign of life.

It came, in the shape of a huge, muscular man with an enormous dog at his heels. He shouted something that she did not catch, in Maltese, she guessed.

'Can you open the gates?' she said,

speaking slowly in case his English was not good. 'I want to turn round.'

He came over scowling. 'Private. Private. You go, or I send dog. Understand?'

The message would have been clear in any language. Faith looked from the man to the dog. It was nearly as big as he was, and almost as threatening. She backed away, apologising.

The door of a shed flew open, and a voice asked something. Another man stood in the open doorway. He had a piece of metal in his hand, and he was hitting his palm with it, menacingly.

'It's OK,' Faith said, hurrying back to the car, 'I'm going. I'm going.'

She started the engine, and propelled by fright, turned the little hatchback more quickly than she would have believed possible. She caught the nearside wing on the stonework as she turned, but she no longer cared. She positively flew up the dusty track, the back wheels leaving the ground altogether as she flung the car around the stoney corners.

Only when she was back on the open road with a view of the sea, did she stop to draw breath and think about what she had seen.

It was the first time since she had been in Malta that she had felt herself to be in actual, physical danger, and the experience had left her breathless and alarmed. But the real shock had not come from the men, nor the dog, nor even the hair-raising drive back up between those narrow walls.

No, what had caused her heart to thump so painfully was what she had glimpsed through the open door behind the man with the metal cosh. Boxes, hundreds of them, in a distinctive deep-blue and silver with a big, black musical note in the centre.

She recognised those boxes, even at that distance. She was quite certain about it. She ought to recognise the design. She had a replica of it in her briefcase. *Moonlight Sonata* — one of the best-selling perfume lines Moonlight Cosmetics had ever produced.

8

Faith's heart was still thudding as she made her way back to the main road. Laval was a good customer and imported thousands of bottles of Moonlight Cosmetics — not only for Malta, but for other places in the Mediterranean. But why store them here — miles from the airport, where every lorry-load was an expedition by ferry? And why the security? Why the threats?

Suddenly, she began to feel alarmed at having shaken off her guide. She wondered what Laval would say, or do, when he learned of it.

Perhaps the best thing was to behave as if nothing had happened. Her mind was still on the events of the day, but she drove to Calypso's Cave and walked around the viewpoint for a moment, then made her way down to the sea.

She would not be conspicuous here. She lay down on a towel on the beautiful beach, and allowed herself to think.

There was a lot to think about. Laval's packaging plant was one of the oddest things of all. There was very little crime on the islands. Laval himself had told her that and Hannibal had said the same thing. Why then was it necessary for him to protect his property with huge mastiffs and muscular men wielding lengths of piping? And why the Moonlight boxes?

Well, she decided, it was not her problem. Tomorrow, she would be safely back at her desk in London, and if there was any difficulty, Brenda could sort it out. Besides, despite her sun cream, her shoulders were getting uncomfortably pink and it was late. She would have to make a swift dash back to the ferry.

She chose the inland route to Sleima, feeling her heart turn over as she saw the shining dome and city walls of

Mdina on the hillside as she passed. Poor Hannibal. Perhaps, after all, he had been right about Laval. If only she could have seen him again, just once, to explain herself, to tell him why she had set off like that without a word. He had wanted that chance, too, she remembered, but then there was the question of last night, seeing him with the little maid.

She sighed. Well, she would probably never see him again. She turned the car into the shade of the oleanders, and parked outside the hotel.

Hannibal was waiting.

He was not smiling as he came towards her, and he took her arm with an urgency which at once thrilled and distressed her.

'Where have you been?'

'Gozo,' she said, as if he had the right to demand an explanation. 'Laval suggested it. He gave me a pass for the ferry.'

Hannibal's face was grim. 'Did he indeed? Faith, we have got to talk. Now.

Before you go back into that hotel, and certainly before you go back to England. It's important.'

'Can't we talk here?'

He did not answer, but gave her a look which spoke volumes.

'Get into the car,' he said. 'Trust me.'

And somehow, looking into those brown eyes, she did trust him, and obeyed.

⋆   ⋆   ⋆

'It's beautiful here,' Faith said.

They were parked on a rugged part of the coast overlooking the sea, and the ground between, although rocky and parched, was alive with the fronds of what looked like fennel and tansy.

But Hannibal, for once, was in no mood to discuss the beauty of the island.

'Never mind that,' he said, abruptly. 'Tell me what you know about Laval.'

'I thought it was you who was going to give me explanations,' Faith said, sitting back in the seat of the car. Today had made her uneasy about Laval, but Hannibal had not been entirely open with her either. After all, he had not even told her that he had once worked for Laval.

To her surprise it was the first thing he said. 'The point is, Faith, I've got nothing concrete to go on. Laval has seen to that. I worked for him at one time.'

'So I heard,' Faith broke in drily.

'Then you probably heard, too, that I was dismissed, for looking through his private papers in the middle of the night?'

She nodded. 'But you didn't do that?'

He met her eyes. 'Oh, yes, I did. At least, I tried to. Stupid of me, I suppose, but I was convinced that he was up to something.'

'What sort of something?'

He shifted uncomfortably. 'That's the trouble. I don't know. I only know that even Laval's hotel and his hire firm, and all his other businesses for that matter, could hardly support him in the life-style he seems to favour. As deputy manager of the hotel, I saw a lot of the paper-work, and I began to notice a lot of things that didn't add up. Signed delivery notes for goods that never arrived. Receipts for guests who never appeared. A hundred and one little things, but it all added up to a pattern. Yet those things in themselves would never account for the sort of money I'm thinking about. I was sure the real problems lay somewhere else entirely. So, when he left his keys one night . . . '

Faith frowned. 'It's a wonder you didn't get arrested.'

He turned to her eagerly. 'Yes, isn't it? But Laval didn't even call the police. He must have been hiding something — I'm more certain of that than ever.'

'But you didn't have the chance to find out what it was?'

'No.' He looked at her intently. 'Faith, just how trustworthy a firm is Moonlight Cosmetics?'

She gaped at him. 'You can't think

that the company was involved. It's not possible. Brenda built the business up from scratch. She's put all her saving into it. No, I just don't believe it. Anyway, there can't be any question of illegal earnings. The company has nearly gone to the wall several times. It's only the last year or two, since Brenda picked up these contracts from the big fashion houses, that we've really started to turn the corner.'

'Contracts?'

She scowled at him. 'There's nothing improper there either — I ought to know, I've been at sales meetings with most of them. Brenda's just brilliant at creating perfumes, and one or two of the big names have commissioned fragrances exclusive to their fashion houses. It's very profitable — their name on the carton gives them an enormous mark-up. But it's perfectly legal, and though it's a good contract of for us, it's the fashion house that makes the real money. It always is. Anyway, Brenda is as straight as a die.'

'You're sure of that?'

His persistence irritated her. 'Look here, Hannibal, I've been working with Brenda day in and day out for months. If there was anything underhand going on, don't you think I'd be the first to know? Just because your Mr Laval is up to no good — which I'm prepared to admit is possible — doesn't mean that Moonlight Cosmetics has to be tarred with the same brush.'

'Even when irregularities in the hotel books often concern reservations made in their name?'

'You're saying that to frighten me.'

He shook his head. 'I'm afraid it is the simple truth. Even your reservation for this trip was not exactly regular.'

'Well, of course it wasn't,' she snapped. 'Nobody could plan on appendicitis. Naturally the reservation had to be changed at the last minute.'

He met her eyes. 'And what reservation was that?'

'Oh, don't be absurd. You know perfectly well what reservation. The one made in the name of Stephanie Rainier. And don't tell me you didn't know about that! I've thought about it a great deal, and I'm convinced that you came to the airport on purpose to meet me — or rather, her. You knew about the hotel, the arrangements, everything. Are you going to deny that?'

'And I thought I had managed it so artfully. You are a difficult woman to fool, Faith Worthing.'

'So you did know about the reservation.'

He shook his head. 'That's just the point. There was no reservation, at least, not on Friday morning. My — someone I know was on duty when somebody rang from Moonlight Cosmetics wanting to change a booking.'

'That would be Brenda,' Faith supplied.

'Well, whoever it was,' Hannibal said, 'there was no booking to be found, and no record of previous reservations either, which the caller said there ought to be. She got quite heated about it, and demanded to talk to the manager, and she was put through to Laval. The next thing we know, the computer system has developed a fault, and no-one can key into it. At lunchtime a man came to repair it, and in the afternoon, hey presto, when the computer is back on line, there is the booking, and half a dozen earlier ones as well.'

'You are joking!'

'Not only that,' Hannibal said, 'but the poor girl on reception gets a dressing-down for her carelessness, and when she protests, Laval promptly takes her off the desk, cuts her pay and demotes her to chambermaid. Says she can't handle responsibility.'

It was obvious that he was talking about the little maid with towels, but Faith's sense of injustice was greater than her jealousy. She sat up so sharply that she banged her head on the roof of the car. 'He can't do that!'

Hannibal regarded her levelly. 'He did.'

'She should have left,' Faith said hotly. 'I would have done!'

'And done what? This is a very small island, and Laval is a powerful man. Without a reference from him she would never have got another job.'

'You managed.'

He laughed bitterly. 'With difficulty, yes. With a foreign employer, as a sort of glorified travel guide. And then only because my boss had had difficulties with Laval himself. He wanted to buy some derelict factory on Gozo and turn it into a holiday complex, but Laval blocked it. Then he heard he'd bought it himself. Probably to build his own apartments.'

No, Faith thought to herself, a packing factory. But for the moment she said nothing. She had more questions to ask of Hannibal Price.

'All right,' she said, 'so your friend found something suspicious about the booking. That doesn't explain that charade at the airport. If Laval had something to hide, you'd have thought he would at least have had that car waiting.'

'That was my doing,' Hannibal said. 'When the booking appeared on the computer, it showed a request for a car hire. It's a service the hotel does provide for guests, at a price — with Laval's firm, of course.'

'Well,' Faith said, 'that's not exactly illegal. I imagine your leisure company offers its customers products which earn it a commission? Laval has just taken that one step further.'

'He takes everything a step further. Me, for instance. He did his best to prevent me from getting a job. And now, he's trying to ensure that I lose it again. He warns all his overseas contacts against my company — and me in particular. That's why I didn't have a client on Monday morning. So I simply cancelled the hire-car booking and went out to meet you myself. I thought at the time, of course, that you were mixed up in this somehow.'

She looked at him closely and asked,

'And now you don't think so?'

He looked at her helplessly. 'What would you have thought? And then, seeing you with Laval — ' He shrugged. 'I decided to keep an eye on you.'

Faith felt her heart sink. 'I see. I thought — I thought perhaps you liked my company.'

He took her head in both his hands and looked into her eyes. 'That's just the trouble, I like it too much. But I was sure that you couldn't be mixed up in anything. And then, when Esperanza told me about the report — '

The gladness which had welled up in her flickered and died.

'Esperanza being your friend, whom you persuaded to search my luggage? Or was that her idea?'

'It was Laval's idea,' he said. 'Rang her while you were actually in his office, I believe. And then made her look in your report — Laval had persuaded her that you were an industrial spy. She agreed because she was afraid of losing her job altogether. Of course, when you complained, she lost her job anyway. That was why she called me last night — to tell me about it. I wish she'd told me before, but she was too afraid of Laval.'

'She's lost her job?' Faith was horrified. 'I shouldn't have said anything, only I thought you'd put her up to it, or she'd done it out of jealousy. I didn't know what to think. But after what I saw with my own eyes today — '

Hannibal interrupted her. 'Jealousy?'

She blushed. 'I saw you together last night.' Even now she couldn't keep the hurt out of her voice. 'You were obviously very close.'

'She was upset,' Hannibal said, and to her amazement, he was laughing. 'And we are a very close family. She's my cousin.'

Faith could only gape at him, gladness leaping in her heart.

'Your cousin,' she breathed. 'I see!'

'So,' he went on, 'what was it you saw with your own eyes today? Or have you been leaping to conclusions again?'

'You were the one who was leaping to conclusions about me!' she retorted. 'But I did see something on Gozo.'

Hannibal listened carefully to her story, and did not interrupt. Only, when she told him about the packing factory, he whistled softly.

'And these boxes you saw, you are sure they were from your firm?'

'*Moonlight Sonata*. I'm absolutely certain of it. The colours are quite distinctive. You couldn't mistake them for anything else.'

Hannibal slapped his knee and sat forward suddenly.

'Of course,' he said suddenly, 'that's it. That's what Laval is up to!'

'What?' Faith asked, mystified.

'Don't you see? The boxes are distinctive. You couldn't mistake them for anything else, you said.'

'Well?'

'Well, supposing the perfume was taken out and packed in different boxes, what then? A box with one of those designer names that you were talking about earlier? Could you mistake it for something else then? And what would the perfume be worth? Three or four times as much?'

'Oh, easily,' Faith said, 'but *Moonlight Sonata* isn't one of the fragrances we sell to the fashion houses. They have their own perfumes created specially.'

'But supposing the customer didn't know that?' Hannibal persisted. 'How could anyone tell?'

'Well, only by sniffing it, or analysing it, I suppose,' Faith said. Despite herself she was beginning to see what Hannibal suggested was possible.

'Are the fashion-house perfumes better?' he wanted to know. 'Do they use more expensive ingredients, things like that?'

'Not really,' Faith said. 'They are all made from the same essences. All perfumes are. It is just the blend that is different. Some oils are more expensive than others, of course, but using only the dearest ones doesn't necessarily make a better perfume. That's down to the perfume-maker's skill. It's only the addition of the name that puts up the price.'

'And suppose that Laval was doing just that? Adding the name by changing the box.'

'It isn't just the box,' Faith objected. 'There's the label, the bottle design, the cap — '

'The bottle?' Hannibal said thoughtfully. 'Yes, you may be right. Decanting every bottle into a new container would hardly be worth the expense. Perhaps we're wrong.'

'Wait a minute though,' Faith said. '*Moonlight Sonata* is a particularly plain bottle. We began with a fancy, cut-glass one, but it didn't really start to sell until we changed it to a plain, square one. It's really only the label and the blue cap that makes it distinctive now.'

'There you are then!' Hannibal said, triumphantly.

Faith was suddenly wary. 'We're only guessing. We've got absolutely nothing to go on. After all, Laval imports our products quite legally. Why shouldn't he have piles of them in store somewhere?'

'In a packaging plant?' Hannibal said scornfully. 'And anyway how many boxes were there?'

'Hundreds I should think. But he does import tens of thousand of bottles. I checked the sales figures before I left London.'

'And that doesn't surprise you? Tens of thousands of bottles on an island this size?'

'But he probably doesn't sell it all here. He has outlets all over the Mediterranean. And not only cosmetics, of course. I think he deals in clothes and food and all sorts of things.'

'And he ships it all through Gozo?' Hannibal said. 'Don't you think that's unusual? I wonder if he does the same thing with everything he imports? Adding value by changing the brand name? A new label in a T-shirt alone could add to its retail value.'

'You think it's as big a racket as that?'

Hannibal looked at her. 'I don't know,' he said. 'But I intend to find out. I have a client to see first thing in the morning, but after that, I'm going to Gozo to have a closer look at that packaging plant. Do you want to come with me? Not right to the plant, of course, that might be dangerous, but if you are somewhere close by, you could keep your own eyes open, and if anything happened — if I didn't come back — you could call the police.'

She thought of the man with the length of metal tubing and shivered.

Then realisation dawned. 'Oh, no, I can't. I go back to London tomorrow.'

She saw the animation drain out of his face, and a look of pain drawn in his eyes. She was miserable herself at the prospect, but perversely, his unhappiness made her heart leap. He did care about her.

'Tomorrow,' he said at last. 'I had forgotten. Could you Fax Brenda, or whatever her name is, and tell her you need a few more days?'

'I might have been able to,' Faith said sadly, 'if I could have taken home a contract. But here's no hope of that.'

'If Laval is defrauding your company, and we can uncover it, that would be more valuable than any contract. Can't you try?'

She looked at him doubtfully. 'Well, Stephanie does it.'

'Ah, yes,' he said, 'the mysterious Stephanie. I wonder if that is another of Laval's little tricks.'

She faced him squarely. 'Stephanie does come to Malta, Hannibal, I know she does. I've seen the orders. I'm carrying letters to our retail outlets here.'

'Well, all I can say is, I was deputy manager of the hotel where she was supposed to have stayed, and I have never heard of her. Not until her name turned up on the computer after that breakdown. So, will you send that Fax?'

She nodded. 'OK, but I don't think

147

Brenda will approve it.'

'It's worth a try. Come on.' He held out a hand to her. 'Let's get something to eat, then I'll take you back to your hotel before you change your mind.'

9

As soon as she got back to the hotel, she sent the Fax and then went to the reception desk to renew her room.

'No problem, madam,' the young woman at the desk said. 'You are very lucky. We had a cancellation earlier in the week of a block booking from Germany, and there are several free rooms.'

'So I heard,' Faith said, and went to her room.

She was awakened the next morning by the telephone. Alert in an instant, she seized the receiver, hoping the caller would be Hannibal.

It was Keith, the Deputy Manager. He was terribly sorry to trouble her, but there had been a mistake over her booking. Would she look in at reception on her way to breakfast?

Perhaps there was a problem in

extending the booking on the firm's account, without Brenda's consent, she thought, as she made her way downstairs.

Keith was waiting for her at the reception desk.

'I'm terribly sorry, Miss Worthing,' he said, as soon as she stepped into the office. 'There seems to have been some mistake. I understand the receptionist last night accepted an extended booking, but I'm afraid that is impossible. There are no rooms available at the hotel for the next fortnight.'

'But I've been told that there was a cancellation.'

He cut her off. 'So there was. In fact, if you had made your request only a half-hour or so earlier we would have been delighted to accommodate you. But when we have a group cancellation like that — which doesn't happen often — we notify our agent immediately, and they include us in their cut-price deals. And this is what happened on this occasion. There is a group of last-minute package-holidaymakers arriving this morning, on the very plane you are due to leave on, I believe. So, the hotel is fully booked, from then on.'

Faith was angry. 'Why wasn't I told this last night?'

The deputy manager said apologetically, 'I don't know. Perhaps the clerk was relying on her memory instead of consulting the read-out for any last-minute amendments. But the booking is there, timed at nine thirty, and I understand from the girl that you didn't attempt to extend your own reservation until after that, just as she was going off duty at ten.'

Faith nodded. 'Yes, it was about ten, but there was no last-minute booking on the computer then. I'm sure of it.'

The deputy manager was looking dangerously flushed. 'I'm afraid I can't account for that, Miss Worthing. You can see with your own eyes the reservation on the screen, and the time we received it is clearly logged. I very much regret having to disappoint you. We should be very pleased, of course, to find you a booking elsewhere . . . '

Faith nodded. 'Very well,' she said, 'perhaps you will do that. And perhaps, under the circumstances, you would also be good enough to telephone the airport and change my flight.'

'And how shall I tell them the account will be settled, madam?'

Faith looked at him quickly. She had been asking herself the same question, but she said confidently, 'Any cost will be paid by my firm. Get them to send an invoice. I believe you have the address.' And she went down to breakfast.

She lingered over her coffee, planning the day ahead. She would have to return the car — and she was not altogether happy about meeting Laval again.

However, Hannibal was due to pick her up at eleven fifteen, as soon as he had finished with his clients. Presumably, the hotel could have no objection if she brought her cases down and waited in the lobby. He would have to take her to her new hotel first.

But it was not to be as simple as that. As she passed the desk on the way up to pack, Keith called her over again.

'I'm terribly sorry, Miss Worthing, but I've been totally unable to get you any accommodation. I've tried every hotel and agency I can think of, and the reply is the same from every one. There are no rooms to be had.'

'But that's impossible,' she cried. 'I've seen notices — '

But even as she spoke she realised that of course it was possible. Laval! He didn't want her to stay on the island. No doubt the young man had his orders. Well, she would see about that! She picked up the desk telephone.

'Get me an outside line!' Here, in full view of the other guests, he could scarcely make difficulties. He did not try to make any. She picked up one of the guidebooks and dialled a hotel number at random. The woman was polite but firm. There had been a last-minute booking, so there was no room available.

After the fourth call, Faith abandoned the attempt. She could not believe that the story about the package deal was true. Perhaps Laval wielded enough influence in this town to ensure that she, Faith Worthing, could obtain no accommodation for that night. She glanced at her watch. Nine-fifteen. The time was getting on. In less than half an hour she should have been catching the bus to the airport. She might still have to catch it if no room was available, she realised. She could hardly sleep on the streets.

'Would you like me to ring the airport?' the senior receptionist asked.

Faith nodded absently and returned to her room to pack. Suddenly, all the excitement of the morning had vanished — there might be no alternative but to return as planned. In all her discussions with Hannibal the night before, this was one scenario they had simply never imagined for a moment. She began to fold her clothes into the suitcase, each garment spelling out for her some incident during these few amazing days she had known Hannibal Price. And now? Unless something remarkable happened soon, it seemed possible that she would never see him again.

The ring of the telephone brought her heart to her mouth, but it was only Reception. There was one seat, it seemed, but not until the following Monday. Did she wish to take it, and cancel her present return flight? The bus to the airport was due to leave, the young man reminded her gently, in just over fifteen minutes, and the airline would make no refund on today's flight. They were holding Monday's tickets until he rang back — what should he tell them?

Faith's mind was in turmoil. 'Give me a moment or two to think,' she said at last. 'I'll get back to you. In the meantime, give me an outside line!'

Hannibal! She must talk to Hannibal. She rang his company, but Mr Price, it seemed, was not in the building. 'He is out arranging a venue for a conference,' a bored voice informed her. 'He called this morning to say that he had an urgent appointment at eleven and would not be back for the rest of the day.'

She slammed down the receiver and called another number.

'One moment please,' Fabio's voice said, and then, a moment later, 'I'm sorry, Mr Laval is in a meeting.'

'But I must speak to him!' Faith insisted, feeling the tears sting her eyes.

Fabio's voice was courteous, but cold. 'I'm sorry, but Mr Laval cannot be disturbed. He left the strictest instructions.'

I'll bet he did, Faith thought to herself furiously. Frantically, she went over her options. There was no flight for days, and no room to be had, and no money to pay for either. She could see no solution but to return to London.

She scrawled a hasty note to Hannibal. It looked cold and formal, and she so much wanted him to know that she was leaving against her will.

On an impulse, she scribbled a post script.

I shall never forgive Laval for what he has done, and most of all for driving us apart. I shall never forget you. These few days have been the happiest of my life. I think I love you. Faith.

For a moment she stared at it and wondered about tearing it up, but then she sealed it into an envelope and wrote his name on it.

Faith finished her packing, took her suitcases to the foyer, and went to the reception desk to sign her invoice.

'If Mr Price comes asking for me, give him this,' Faith said, handing the envelope to the receptionist.

The girl took it without glancing up. 'Next,' she said, taking Faith's key. And that was that. Faith went over to her suitcase and waited, feeling miserable.

'Bus to the airport!' A driver was

standing at the entrance, a list of names in his hand. Faith joined the queue of people waiting to board the bus.

'Miss Worthing?' The receptionist called her name, just as she was about to climb the steps. 'A Fax has just arrived for you,' the girl said.

It was from Brenda, and it was to the point. *Impossible you should extend your stay. Return to London at once.*

'You coming, lady?' the driver wanted to know. Faith nodded slowly and made her way, reluctantly, on to the coach.

The trip to the airport was a nightmare of memories and regrets, and all the way her eyes scanned the road, hoping for a glimpse of Hannibal's car but there was no sign of it. Even at the terminal she loitered until the last minute, hoping against hope that he might somehow rescue her at the eleventh hour.

'Will Miss Faith Worthing, last remaining passenger to London, kindly go to desk fourteen? Final call for Miss Faith Worthing, passenger to London.'

She went unwillingly to the desk, and swung her suitcase on to the baggage weigh. 'Faith Worthing,' she said, then turned when a voice said her name.

'Faith, I thought I'd missed you,' Hannibal said and took her into his arms . . .

*   *   *

'Brenda will be furious,' she said, for the umpteenth time. They were sitting in a café at St Julian, overlooking the sea, and sipping hot, strong coffee. Faith's bag was in Hannibal's car, parked outside, and the plane she should have caught was halfway to London.

'She told me to come straight back to England. I shouldn't have stayed. I've got no money, and nowhere to stay.'

Hannibal grinned at her, happily. 'You forget,' he said, 'you are speaking to a man with contacts in the leisure world. I think I can fix you up with accommodation. Would a suite be acceptable?'

She gave him a rueful smile. 'And how am I supposed to pay for it? I am a fool. I should have caught that plane.'

He went on grinning. 'No, I think we can manage it. There's a hospitality suite which we keep for members of the management, and other overseas visitors. The company sometimes flies people over, tour operators and so on, and puts them up for a day or two, provided that they are prospective clients, and likely to put our leisure facilities in their brochure!'

'Well, I'm hardly a prospective client. And I couldn't pay for a suite, either, however long you gave me. Not on my salary.'

'Yes, but not everybody decides that our kind of holiday activities will suit their customers. A lot don't take us on, even when they come to see it. You'll have to sign the visitor's book, saying that you are a foreign representative, that's all. After all, that is exactly what you are!'

She gazed at him. 'It can't be that easy.'

He laughed. 'Well, not usually. But if I tell them that you cancelled your flight home in order to have a conference with me, I don't think there'll be a problem. I'm pretty well my own boss these days. So, let me take you to my parlour.'

He paid the bill and she followed him out to the car.

'But won't Laval tell them something different?'

Hannibal gave a sharp laugh. 'I told you, my employer doesn't see eye to eye with Laval after that business about the factory site. Besides, Laval thinks you are on that plane. That's to our advantage, at least for a few hours. He can't make life difficult if he doesn't know you're here.'

'Well, I suppose so,' Faith said. 'But I'm still not sure that I like the idea of camping out in your accommodation.'

'The hospitality facility is hardly camping out,' Hannibal said. 'Anyway, do you have any better ideas?'

She shook her head.

'Well then, climb in.' He turned the car up the hill to where a scatter of new buildings nestled among a forest of palms and oleanders. Faith looked around in amazement. There was a complex of swimming pools, with water slides and diving pools, and an ornamental lake. There was a small golf course, too, and a pair of tennis courts, and what looked almost like an ice-rink, but Hannibal told her it was for miniature go-kart racing.

'A leisure complex, you see,' Hannibal said. 'Activity holidays. We have a lecture room, too — and a studio. People can come and do a fortnight on the antiquities, or lace-making. You name it. I think it will become a major attraction. The hospitality suite is down here, over the ballroom and the restaurants.'

She followed him down the uneven

path to where a glistening, new building rose, its hundred windows each looking out on to the distant sea. On the top story was a small balcony, furnished with bushes in tubs and colourful patio chairs. Hannibal followed her gaze.

'Yes,' he said, nodding proudly. 'That's it. Come inside.'

The cool, elegant foyer seemed a million miles from the dusty chaos of the island outside. Pot plants nodded in every corner, and the green, stone floor shone with a beautiful lustre. In the corner, a lift like a gilded cage wafted to the ground, beside an ornamental pool with a wooden bridge and a little waterfall.

'Nice, isn't it?' Hannibal said, and led the way to the lift.

The hospitality apartment was on the top floor, and furnished in the same vein. In the bathroom was a three-cornered tub with gilt taps shaped like dolphins and a Jacuzzi. The sitting-room was full of leather furniture, oak dressers and decanters full of every imaginable drink. It was quite a relief to open the french windows on to the balcony, and be reassured by the sturdy ordinariness of the patio chairs and table. Faith sank down on one of the chairs.

'Think you'll be OK here?' Hannibal asked, coming out to join her. 'Only, we ought to get a move on if we want to get to Gozo this afternoon.'

In all the excitement she had half-forgotten the projected trip to Gozo, but at his words she slipped off her chair at once. 'Let's go,' she said.

It was well into the afternoon before they reached Gozo. Hannibal had bought a snack on the ferry, and they didn't stop until they had reached the narrow track where Faith had taken a wrong turning the previous day.

'Along here somewhere,' Faith said. 'I found some road-works at a corner.'

'I think I know where it is,' Hannibal said. 'I'll take you to the beach first. You sit in the sun and enjoy yourself. If I'm not back in two hours, go into the hotel and telephone this number.' He slipped a piece of paper into her hand.

'But I was coming with you,' she protested.

'Not to the factory. That's too dangerous. Besides we don't want Laval and his merry men to know you're here. No, you stay here and wait. I won't be long.'

And before she had time to protest, he had turned the car in a screech of tyres, and was gone.

10

Faith watched the time anxiously, but it was less than forty-five minutes before Hannibal returned, his face like thunder. Faith saw him striding down the beach, and was struck again by how handsome he was, his dark skin luminous against the pale-blue silk of his shirt. She got up to greet him.

'What happened? Did you find anything?'

He threw her a glance of pure frustration. 'That's just the point. Nothing happened. The place is deserted — there was nothing to find.'

She stared at him in disbelief. 'But it can't be! I saw it.' A thought struck her. 'You do believe me, don't you?'

Hannibal nodded. 'Oh, yes, I believe you,' he said savagely. 'It is obvious the place has only just been vacated. Tyre tracks everywhere, stacks of empty crates piled up outside the warehouses, and signs that somebody had had the most enormous bonfire. The ashes were still warm.'

'You went in?' She could hardly believe it.

He gave a short laugh. 'It wasn't difficult. The gates were open, and every door in the place was left hanging ajar. All the machinery has been moved. You can see the marks on the floor where the machines stood, and where the dust had collected behind them. And amongst all the rubbish lying around there is not a single piece of paper or cardboard to indicate what had been going on there. Anyone passing might suppose it had simply been used as a store.'

'Laval must have worked quickly,' Faith said.

'He must have worked all night,' Hannibal said, 'which proves one thing. Your threat to stay must have worried him badly. He tried to force you to return to London, but he was taking no chances. I'm even more convinced that there was something here to hide.'

'Perhaps he thought that I would tell Brenda what I'd seen,' Faith said thoughtfully. 'Something like that. He must have known that it was impossible for me to stay in Malta without a room.'

Hannibal slipped an arm around her waist, and looked down at her gently.

'But he couldn't be sure of that, could he? You can see what he must have suspected — that I would invite you to share my flat with me.'

The thought, for some reason, had not occurred to her, but now that it did, it took her breath away, and she felt the blood course through her veins.

'I might have asked you, too,' Hannibal continued, 'but there is already a guest in my house. Would you have been insulted?'

She shook her head, feeling her cheeks flush. 'I should have liked it.'

'You meant it then, what you wrote in that note?'

She mouthed the word yes, but never spoke it, for his lips were already closing on hers.

It seemed a long moment before he said, 'We must get back. It would be best to get you in the apartment before nightfall.'

'And you have a guest,' she reminded him lightly.

He smiled, a little embarrassed. 'Only a relation. A cousin. There is no problem for me. But it is wise, I think, if you are safely in the suite as soon as possible. Laval will soon discover that you did not board that plane.'

The thought of Laval searching for her on such a small island was not a comfortable one. True, she was a free agent, and, short of physical violence, there was little he could do to prevent her doing as she pleased. But, remembering the men and the dog, she was not altogether certain that Laval would stop short of physical violence.

She said, ruefully, 'And you found nothing at all at the fireworks factory?'

'Only this,' Hannibal said. 'It was on the remains of the bonfire. It is scorched, but the flames hadn't quite reached it. It may tell us something.'

It was a small piece of torn card, about the size of a twenty-pound note, and although the edge was blackened and curled, it was easy to see that it had once formed part of a small box. The design had been damaged by fire, but part of it was still clearly visible, a golden sun vanishing into a pool of blood-red sea, and the four letters CAES picked out in gold lettering.'

Faith looked at it for a moment, and then said, with certainty, 'I know what this is! *De Caesario*. You know, the fashion house that won all the awards last year. This is their logo. They launched a perfume in the spring, made under licence by one of the really big perfume houses in France, I think.'

Hannibal looked at her intently. 'Expensive?'

'Extremely expensive. And exclusive. Supply was deliberately kept limited to make it more desirable.'

'And don't you think it is interesting,' Hannibal said, 'that we should find a box for it on Laval's land? What did it smell like?'

'I've no idea,' Faith said. 'I shouldn't think many people have.'

Hannibal's face clouded, and then he said, 'Faith, are you prepared to take a risk? To expose Laval?'

'A risk,' she said. 'What kind of risk?'

'I'd like you to spend the evening telephoning. There's a phone in your apartment. Ring up all the stores in Malta that sell perfume,. You'll find a list of the best stores in the publicity brochure. Ring them up and say you are looking for the *de Caesaris*, or whatever it is.'

'*De Caesario*,' Faith corrected. 'And what do you want me to do if I find it?'

'Buy some,' Hannibal said, 'though I'd better send Esperanza out tomorrow to make the actual purchase. I'll ring you tonight to see how you have got on. Then when we find some, you can see what it smells like.'

'It will be expensive,' Faith said.

Hannibal smiled. 'Let me worry about that. It will be worth a little expense to test my theory.'

★ ★ ★

The journey back to the ferryport was uneventful, although Faith was aware of Hannibal's watchfulness. It made her feel increasingly uneasy, and she began to wish that Hannibal's car was a little less conspicuous.

Hannibal must have had a similar thought because, as they were going down to the car deck again, he put his hand out to a swarthy man in a tattered shirt.

'Thomaso! My old friend!'

The man turned, surprised. 'Hannibal!'

Hannibal leaned forward and murmured something as they moved down the stairway. He spoke softly, but Faith could hear enough to know that the conversation was not in English.

The man listened intently, and cast a doubtful look in Faith's direction, but at last he nodded reluctantly.

'Right,' Hannibal said to Faith, 'Thomaso will take you to the apartment. We are lucky to have met him. It's safer for you than travelling in my car. If Laval is looking for you, he will never think of Thomaso's van! Go with him now.'

Faith was ready to protest, but the man he called Thomaso had her arm in a vice-like grip.

'Come!' he said, and led the way to an ancient van, so battered and buckled it seemed a wonder that it ever moved at all, but the swarthy man coaxed it into life and it rattled and shook its way off the ship and out on to the roads of Malta.

Faith was seized by sudden panic. For the second time in a week she found herself being driven by a man she had never met.

'Where are you taking me?' she gasped.

He did not even glance in her direction. 'Is leisure park. Is OK.'

Faith felt a little reassured, but she was still unhappy by the sudden turn of events. She had been swept into this van almost before she knew it.

'How do you know Hannibal?' she asked. 'Did you know he was going to Gozo?' Spectres of kidnap were rising in her mind.

Thomaso turned to give her a withering glance. 'I friend of Esperanza. Hannibal say me she in trouble. I help. Is all.'

'Esperanza,' Faith said with relief. 'Hannibal's cousin. I see.'

'Cousin!' The man opened his window and spat savagely on to the road. 'Not so bad for me if he only her cousin. In Malta are many cousins. But he more than cousin to Esperanza. I want marry her — but he don't like this, I think. And she — she love him too much.'

Faith went cold. Had she been right in her suspicions the other night, after all? 'And he loves her?' she said, trying to keep her voice steady.

The man's frown deepened. 'Oh, yes, they like this!' He took his hands from the steering-wheel to interlock two fingers. If his words had not brought her heart to her mouth, the gesture would have done, as cars swirled past on both sides, horns blaring. But Thomaso was concerned only with his message. He took the wheel again.

'He worry for her. She worry for him. She don't like he has English woman stay in hospitality. But maybe now I take you, I tell her — she listen to me — marry me. I don't know. I got good boat. I fish. I make good husband.'

Faith sat back in the rattling van and closed her eyes. So, Hannibal loved Esperanza, and she loved him. Of course, cousin could have a hundred meanings, especially in a society which had wide family ties — and it was possible, surely, to marry your cousin.

Remarks which Hannibal had made drifted back to her, falling into place like pieces of a jigsaw.

'There is already a guest in my house, a relation.' Of course! Esperanza had lost her job at the hotel. Presumably she had lost her accommodation, too. Who but her cousin would offer her a room? You are leaping to conclusions she told herself — but she couldn't shake off the feeling that Esperanza meant more to Hannibal then Faith ever could.

What was she doing here — chasing rainbows? She had heard a hundred stories about holiday romances. She should have known better.

'Lady,' Thomaso's voice was plaintive, 'I got to go. You get out now?'

Faith opened her eyes with a start, and realised that they were back at the leisure park.

She managed a wan smile as she thanked Thomaso, and watched him drive away, the van lurching treacherously over the uneven ground.

Then she turned and went back into the suite. The man at the security desk recognised her and greeted her with a curt nod, and she went up in the lift and let herself in with her electronic key.

She poured herself a drink from one of the decanters and flung herself down on a big, white sofa. Hannibal had misled her.

Or had he? He'd never said anything, she thought suddenly, which could lead her to suppose that there was anything serious in his intentions. He had said that he found her attractive, but it was she, herself, who had declared her feelings and had interpreted his kisses as something more than flirtation. For the first time in her life, she had allowed herself to fall helplessly in love.

And perhaps worst of all, if Thomaso was to be believed, she was not even the first of his flirtations. Esperanza did not like it when Hannibal had an English woman in this suite.

She drained her glass and wandered

into the kitchen. There were frozen foods in the freezer and a small microwave oven, and she soon managed a light meal, but the food tasted like dust in her mouth, and she hardly ate any of it. At last she pushed her plate away, and made her way to the gold-plated telephone.

She had been a fool to stay, certainly, but if Laval was cheating Brenda and the firm, she could at least salvage something by trying to uncover that. There was a glossy brochure by the phone, advertising the highspots of Malta, and a file of cuttings and photographs showing the leisure complex in various stages of development. She picked up the brochure. These must be the outlets Hannibal wanted her to ring. She glanced at her watch.

There was just time. She picked up the telephone and began to dial.

She had the story worked out in advance. She was an English visitor, attempting to find a present to take home for a friend. Did they by any

178

chance stock an exclusive perfume called *de Caesario*? Or, she added on a sudden impulse, a slightly less-expensive one named *Moonlight Sonata*?

The first call gained her nothing. No, they could not offer *de Caesario*. They might be able to order one of the special gift-packs — perfume and nightgown, but it would take some time to arrive. *Moonlight Sonata*? They did stock it sometimes — they might have one somewhere. When was the lady coming in?

The second call was much the same, and the third, and the fourth, although the gift-pack varied. Perfume and silk blouse, perfume and T-shirt. Two boutiques could offer *Moonlight Sonata*, most others had never stocked it.

When Hannibal rang she passed on the news, such as it was. 'Not much help, I'm afraid.' It was an effort to keep her voice light, but she managed it.

Hannibal sounded anxious. 'I'm interested in these gift-packs. Didn't you tell me Laval also traded in clothing? He may be doing the same thing elsewhere. And odd, don't you think, that when Laval imports tens of thousands of bottles of *Moonlight Sonata*, you could find so few bottles on the island? He must have been anxious not to let the perfume become known.'

'Do you want me to order one of these gift-packs?'

'No, you stay where you are for now,' Hannibal said thoughtfully. 'Esperanza and I will see what we can find tomorrow. I'll come to see you in the evening, and let you know what we have found. Can you look after yourself till then? Go to the beach or something, but keep a low profile. Good-night, my darling. I shall always remember today.'

So shall I, Faith thought bitterly. So Hannibal and Esperanza were to go shopping, while she remained cooped up here, or skulked about on the beach trying not to be recognised. And she didn't even have Hannibal's telephone number should she need to contact him.

Perhaps it was in the publicity brochure. She picked up up, and began to glance through it.

Photographs of the site before development commenced. The first water-slide completed. Close-ups of the lift and the waterfall in the foyer. Plans of the golf-course and development yet to come. And then, pictures of the staff — a party for the opening of the leisure park, held, Faith noted with a grim smile, at the Cranmore Hotel. She looked at the picture more closely.

Yes, there he was, grinning happily, sitting at a table with his arms around two women whom he was pulling towards him, into the picture. Hannibal Price. Her eyes misted over, and then a little shiver ran down her spine.

One of the women was a tall, striking blonde whom Faith had never seen. The other was Stephanie Rainier.

It was too much. Faith reached out a shaking hand for the receiver, and dialled a London number.

'I want to speak to Charles Chatcombe.'

11

Charles came to the phone almost immediately. 'Fay, darling, what on earth happened to you? I waited for your plane to arrive . . . '

'Yes, Charles, I know — ' Faith interrupted but Charles talked on.

'Are you in trouble again?' he asked, sounding as though he was talking to a rather backward child.

'No, Charles, not really . . . ' Faith began and explained what had been happening. She tried not to let her emotions come through in her voice. If Charles realised that Faith had fallen in love with Hannibal, she felt he might actually explode, so she said, 'You don't believe any of this about Laval?'

Charles snorted. 'Jean-Baptiste Laval is an international trader. Our company does business with him. Would you really take the word of a young fly-by-night, over the word of an important businessman? Really, Fay, you are more naïve than I took you for. Still, at your age, you can't be expected to have much experience of the world. No, my dear, you take my word for it. It's Hannibal Price you should be wary of.'

Faith thought of the photograph she had seen in the publicity file. Yes, perhaps Charles was right.

'But the factory. Why was it closed down if Laval had nothing to hide?'

'How do you know it was closed down? Because Hannibal told you so? You didn't see it with your own eyes. And that piece of card — he could have found it anywhere, or had it in his pocket ready to produce at the critical moment. No, my guess is that the factory, or the packing plant, or whatever it is, is still there, in full operation.'

'But why the dogs, and the barbed wire if it is just a warehouse?'

'Fay, darling,' Charles said, 'you said

yourself that there must be thousands of pounds worth of goods there. And supposing someone had a grievance. Your Hannibal for example.'

'He's not my Hannibal,' she said, bitterly. 'But why would he go to all this trouble? What would he have to gain?'

'Inveigling you into his clutches for one thing, my girl — and persuading you to throw yourself on his mercy like this. Tucked away there, and nobody knowing about it! Anything could have happened. And any doubts he can raise about Laval are likely to do a certain amount of harm, even if they are proved to be groundless. No smoke without fire — a lot of international businessmen feel that. Besides, if he could persuade you to stop Moonlight Cosmetics from supplying Laval, that would be a small blow in its own right. He's obviously got a grudge against the man for catching him with his hands in the till.'

'It wasn't the till — ' Faith began, but her voice trailed off. She had, she realised, only Hannibal's own word for that.

'Laval shouldn't have let the fellow get off so lightly,' Charles went on, as though she hadn't spoken. 'Giving them a talking-to, and then letting them go never does any good in the end. Should have had the police in at once.'

Faith felt cold and sick with disappointment and shame. Charles was so rational, and what he said made her feel like a six-year-old. Of course, if you looked at it that way, Charles was quite right. And Laval had never been less than charming to her. Why had she suddenly decided to cast him as a villain?

'This Hannibal fellow probably talked him out of it.' Charles was pursuing his own train of thought. 'Terribly plausible, these chaps. And accomplished liars.'

Like telling me he had never heard of Stephanie Ranier, she thought miserably. 'I've been a fool, Charles,' she said.

Charles seemed to consider this, and there was a moment's silence. Then, when he spoke, his voice was warmer. 'No, my dear Fay, I can hardly blame you. If this fellow can fool a man like Laval, who knows something about the world, then I can hardly blame you for falling for his line. The trouble is, Fay, you need someone to protect you. This rushing around the world on sales trips, it's all very well for some, but you are just not cut out for it. You are too — ' He searched for the word. 'Too trusting. You did the right thing in ringing me. Don't worry any more. I'll see that you get a credit card. I'll get in touch with the airport, and I'll explain matters to Brenda. In the meantime, give me your phone number and don't move from there on any account.'

'But Hannibal — ' she began.

'Make some excuse. Tell him you have a headache and can't go out. Anything. Just stay there until I contact you. Leave everything to me, and try to get some sleep.'

★ ★ ★

It was late before Faith awoke. The sun was already high in the sky, and the island and the sea shimmered with a thousand colours, oblivious to the darkness in her soul.

She forced down a cup of coffee and sat on the balcony, watching the traffic come and go on the main coast road beneath her. Out to sea, little coloured fishing-boats twinkled as they rose and fell and the pleasure cruisers skimmed like white swans across the water. Beautiful, she thought, beautiful, cruel and deceptive, like Hannibal Price.

But he would be here, later. She prepared herself with a mental barrage of things to say. She was not well. She was tired. She was waiting for a call from London — that much at least was true. She would manage somehow to escape his questioning, and ensure that she had a place to sleep between now and Monday. She could even tackle him about the document he had persuaded her to sign. She could handle it, she told herself, provided he did not attempt to take her in his arms. She didn't think that she could cope with that.

She didn't go to the beach as he had suggested. She simply sat, holding her cooling coffee cup, watching the passing island with unseeing eyes.

The telephone bell disturbed her. Hannibal! She went back into the apartment and lifted the receiver.

'Mr Price for you,' the security guard said.

She could feel the little prickles of apprehension lifting the hairs on her neck, as she said, as coolly as she could, 'Put him on.'

It was absurd, the way her heart was pounding. He was a cheat, she told herself firmly, a liar and a cheat. He had deceived her. Well, now it was her turn. Hannibal must not detect that there was any change in her attitude towards him. Well, he would find that she was as good an actor as he was.

'Faith?' His voice was warm, like a caress.

'Hello, Hannibal.' Her own voice sounded unnaturally bright and brittle, even to her own ears. Surely he would detect that something was wrong. But he didn't seem to notice.

'Look, my love, we're finding it difficult to locate any of these *de Caesario* gift packs, but it seems that there is a chance we might find one at the Craft Village in the centre of the island. I'm going there now, and as soon as I've finished I'll come and pick you up. We could have a picnic, Maltese style.'

'Oh,' she said hastily, 'I couldn't go out. I'm too tired.'

'You are?' He was an accomplished actor. His voice betrayed only loving concern. 'I'm sorry, Faith. This must be difficult for you. I'll be as quick as I can.'

No, that was not at all what she intended. She didn't want him to come.

'Why don't you take Esperanza for a

picnic?' she suggested.

'Oh!' This time he did sound taken aback — surprised rather than embarrassed. 'Yes. Yes, Faith. That is a nice idea. I think perhaps I will.'

It was not the response she had expected. 'Perhaps she'll make the picnic for you,' she suggested, coating her voice with saccharine sweetness.

'Yes,' Hannibal said again. 'She'd like that. Nice of you to think of it. I'll see you later then.'

'Splendid!' Faith said, and this time she could not keep the bitterness out of her voice.

'Faith, my love, are you all right?'

'I told you, I'm very tired.'

'Poor Faith. I shouldn't be more than an hour or two.'

An hour or two. It was a lifetime to fill, and yet she dreaded the time when it would be over. She could pass some time at least by pretending to eat some lunch. She heated some lasagne in the microwave, and chased it around her plate. The buzzer from reception roused her.

She glanced at her watch. It was less than an hour since Hannibal had rung.

'Visitor for you, Miss Worthing.'

There was nothing for it. 'Send him up,' she said, and a few moments later the doorbell sounded. She pushed the intercom button.

'Hello.'

'Faith?' The voice sounded oddly strained.

'Just push,' she said wearily.

The door opened, and her visitor came into the room.

'Fay,' Charles Chatcombe said, 'you don't sound very pleased to see me! I caught the first plane this morning. As I told you last night, a firm like ours usually merits a few privileges.'

He sat in the deepest armchair, and helped himself to a large port from the nearby decanter. He had not been in the flat above a moment or two, and already he had clearly taken charge.

'I thought the safest way of delivering your credit card was to bring it myself,' he said, with an expression which could only be described as smug. 'That way I could be certain that you would come home sensibly, and not allow yourself to be drawn into any more hare-brained schemes.'

She tried to think of something sensible to say, but couldn't.

'Still, I am very pleased that you seemed to be seeing sense at last,' Charles said graciously. 'I've spoken to Brenda, and she agrees that, provided you pay your own fare and no lasting harm is done, she will overlook the incident. Not that, I think, you will ever get an overseas assignment again.'

'But does she understand why I stayed?' Faith asked, in an agonised voice. 'She knows I was doing it for the company.'

Charles favoured her with a withering look. 'My dear Fay, you told her you needed more time. She thinks you are merely overzealous. I saw no future in persuading her that you are actually overgullible. Of course I did not pass on your preposterous rumours. And Laval has actually agreed to Fax a small order to London for *Mediterranean Moonlight*. Only a dozen or so bottles, but he will negotiate with the real sales representative later — so Brenda will no doubt feel that your belated return was in part justified.'

She gaped at him again. 'How did you manage that?'

'Oh,' Charles said airily, 'pulled a few strings. Reminded him of a few favours he owed to my company.'

'You've spoken to Laval?'

'Why, yes,' Charles said. 'Telephoned him from the airport. Apologised on your behalf, of course. Must say he was very charming about it. Even managed to find me a couple of return tickets to London this afternoon. So, if you are quite ready, we could get back straight away. I've a taxi coming in twenty minutes.'

'But Hannibal — ' she began.

'Leave him a note,' Charles said. 'Or I will.'

'No,' she said, 'I'll do that myself. You could pack my case if you like. There's not much to do — I've only taken a few things out of it.'

Charles went off into the bedroom, while she took out a piece of paper and wrote a note to Hannibal — the hardest words she had ever written.

Have gone back to England with Charles. Realised you could not be trusted when I saw you with Stephanie. Charles says that staying here and signing a visitors' book at your invitation gives you no hold over me in law, so do not feel that your little scheme has worked. Next time you try to trick someone, be a little more careful with your publicity folder! Faith.

She looked at the words, and then folded the paper and placed it prominently on the centre of the table.

'Are we ready then?' Charles said, bringing in her suitcase and her briefcase. 'I've checked the list, and everything's packed — though why you threw your things together in that haphazard fashion, I can't imagine. I had to repack the whole case from scratch.'

'I was in a hurry, Charles,' she said meekly. She looked around the luxurious room. It had been an adventure, while it lasted. 'Ready when you are,' she said.

He gave that cat-with-the-cream smile of his. 'Right. The taxi will be here in a moment to take us to the airport — and speaking of airports, I brought something for you. A touch of luxury — a cut above the things your funny, little company turns out.'

He handed her a gift-wrapped package, and she undid it, clumsily. Then abruptly, she stiffened, gazing at the gold-embossed package in her hand.

'Well, aren't you going to open it?' he said. 'It's the sort of present you could take for granted, Fay, if you'd only marry me.'

She slipped open the cardboard lid,

and let the bottle slide on to her palm. It was an ornate bottle, flask-shaped with two handles and a golden clasp. A last, forlorn ray of hope flickered and died. Almost absently she took off the lid and touched the fragrance to the pulse point of her wrist. And joy, dizzying wonderful joy rose in her heart.

'Wonderful!' she breathed.

'Glad you like it,' Charles said. 'Rather expensive, but what does that matter when a gift gives pleasure.'

Faith lifted her eyes to his. 'No, Charles. This is wonderful because this is not *de Caesario*. I'd know this smell anywhere — it's *Moonlight Sonata*. It's true. It's all true. I'm afraid you have been conned.'

And sitting on the side of the suitcase, she began to laugh.

12

She was still laughing when the entry-phone rang. She stood up at once.

'That'll be Hannibal,' she said, her heart dancing.

'Well,' Charles said, tetchily, 'if you are going to sit there laughing like an idiot, I'll let him in myself, since clearly you have lost your senses completely.' He strode to the door and opened it. 'Come in, come in, you and your lady friend.'

Faith whirled around. Yes, indeed, Esperanza was there, clutching a picnic bag, and behind her, neatly dressed today and smiling foolishly, was Thomaso.

'Thomaso!' Faith said. 'Come in.'

'Yes,' Charles said, 'do, do. Don't mind me. We only have a plane to catch.'

'Charles!' Faith said gently, 'Don't be disagreeable.'

She turned to Thomaso. 'I was expecting Hannibal.'

'He coming,' Thomaso said, smiling crookedly. 'Only can't park. Taxi in way.'

'There you are, Fay. That's our taxi. My dear girl, if we don't get a move on we shall miss the plane.'

'Plane?' Hannibal had appeared at the doorway. Faith felt her heartbeat quicken at the sight of him, so tanned and athletic and handsome. Somehow he seemed to breathe air and sea and sunshine. Beside him, Charles appeared a thing of gloomy corridors and dusty files. 'Faith are you going somewhere?'

'She is coming home with me,' Charles said.

Hannibal shot him a glance full of angry hurt. 'You are Charles?'

'You've heard of me, at least!' Charles said. 'I thought perhaps Fay had forgotten my existence until she needed protection.'

'Hannibal!' Faith made herself heard at last. 'Look at this!' She held out the bottle of *de Caesario*. 'This is it. The proof you needed. The perfume in this bottle is *Moonlight Sonata* — just as we thought. Charles bought it from the airport. So, I'll take it back to Brenda and the whole thing will be made public. Your name will be cleared. You'll be able to marry — ' She had been about to say Esperanza, but the girl was holding hands with Thomaso, and the words died on Faith's lips. ' — anyone you like,' she finished shakily.

Hannibal held her eyes steadily, 'But will the person I like marry me, or will she go back to England with this Charles?'

It was a moment or two before Faith could take in that this was a proposal of marriage. 'And what about Esperanza?'

'Esperanza! What does she have to do with it?'

'You love her. Thomaso said so. And she loves you.'

'Well, of course I love her,' Hannibal

said. 'She is like a sister to me.'

'I tell you,' Thomaso said indignantly. 'More than a cousin. When I want to marry Esperanza, have to ask Hannibal. And,' he went on with a huge grin splitting his face, 'Hannibal say yes.'

So that was it, Faith thought. But there was something else she wanted to know. 'So, what about Stephanie?' she demanded.

Hannibal shook his head, 'I told you, I have never heard of Stephanie.'

'Don't lie to me, Hannibal. I've seen a photograph of you together!'

'Where?' he demanded.

'In the publicity file.'

'Show me!'

She seized the file and opened it at the photograph. All her feelings of mistrust returned as she thrust it towards him. 'There!'

He looked at the book, and frowned slightly. 'That's Anna Lindstrom. She's the wife of the developer. She stays here sometimes. Esperanza was very worried when I put you in the hospitality suite

— she was convinced Anna was coming this week.'

'I tell her that,' Thomaso said. 'Esperanza say it bad when you have English woman in flat.'

'That is Anna Lindstrom?' Faith said, pointing.

Hannibal looked at her blankly. 'No,' he said. 'The blonde lady is Anna Lindstrom. The woman you are pointing at is Veronique Laval — the wife of Jean-Baptiste Laval.'

There was a moment's stunned silence, and Hannibal said softly, 'I see!'

Their eyes met in perfect understanding.

'Fay, my dear girl,' Charles put in loudly, 'are you coming on this plane with me or not?'

'But don't you see, Charles? Laval has been working a fraud with his wife. She has been shopping him huge quantities of *Moonlight Sonata*, and he has been repacking it and shipping it out at ten times the price. A very neat, little swindle. And I wouldn't mind

202

betting that the nightgowns and T-shirts in the special presentation packs have never seen the inside of *de Caesario* either. Though how it was ever economical to transfer the perfume into different bottles I shall never know.'

'Let me see that bottle,' Hannibal said, and she handed it over. He took it in his two hands and gently rubbed his thumbs across the surface.

'There,' he said, 'there is your answer. The perfume hasn't been rebottled — the original square bottle has simply been slipped inside a second skin.' He eased the two sections apart gently. 'So Laval kills two birds with one stone. The outer skin made a perfect disguise, and at the same time made the perfume bottle seem bigger.'

'No wonder Stephanie was so keen on changing the shape of the original bottle,' Faith said slowly. 'She insisted that the simpler shape would sell better, and Laval saw to it that she was right. And, of course, Laval did not want to sign a large contract with me until he had seen a full-size sample. We are having another battle about the shape of the new *Mediterranean Moonlight* flask. Brenda had designed a pretty, circular bottle, but Stephanie was arguing fiercely for a simple, cylindrical shape.'

'Which would no doubt have been given a new casing,' Hannibal said grimly.

'No wonder he wouldn't sign a contract with me,' Faith said. 'He would have been committed to buying a consignment of the stuff in the circular bottle and that was the last thing he wanted.'

'And, of course, he didn't want you to spend time with me,' Hannibal put in. 'He knew I was suspicious of him, and he can't have been certain what I had found amongst his papers at the hotel. He did everything he could to prevent us spending any time together.'

'What I don't understand,' Faith said, 'is why there was all that trouble with the hotel booking. Stephanie certainly came here, we know that.'

Hannibal laughed. 'You don't put your wife in a hotel when you own a magnificent villa five miles away. No, that was the one weak spot in their plan. He should never have tried to give Veronique false invoices for her pretend visits to the Cranmore. If he hadn't done that, I would never have got on to him.'

'I wonder why he did?' Faith said.

'Petty greed, I imagine,' Hannibal said. 'They were swindling people out of thousands of pounds, but they could not bear to lose the hundred or two that Veronique — Stephanie — could claim back as expenses.'

'Fay,' Charles said, in the tone of a man whose patience was rapidly being exhausted, 'are you coming home with me or not?'

'How can I come?' Faith protested. 'What about exposing Laval?'

'I'm sure your young gentleman friend here is more than capable of dealing with that. Hand it over to the

205

police, or some appropriate agency. He doesn't need you.'

'Of course he needs me,' Faith said. 'I'm the only one who can identify the perfume. I'm a vital witness.'

'Faith,' Charles said, using her full name for a change, 'you cannot seriously intend to get yourself mixed up in this unsavoury business. There could be trials and court appearances, and all kinds of unpleasantness. I have no wish to be associated with it — or for you to be associated with it either.'

'Charles, we are talking about major fraud here. This man has implicated Brenda in something which could have ruined the company. You can't just wash your hands of it.'

Charles drew himself up to his full height. 'A man in my position cannot afford adverse publicity,' he said. 'Our company has dealings with Laval.'

'What has that got to do with it?'

'It has everything to do with it. Now, are you coming home with me or not?'

Faith looked from Charles to Hannibal, and from Hannibal to Esperanza and Thomaso who were standing on the balcony, so lost in each other that they were oblivious to the discussion in the apartment. 'Perhaps I had better go,' she said to Hannibal. 'I'd better warn Brenda.'

'Call her,' Hannibal said, not moving a muscle. 'Get her to come and see for herself.'

Faith looked at him. 'Perhaps I will.'

Charles gave them a withering glance. 'Well, Faith, I'll leave you to your foolishness. I must say, after this performance, I am not altogether sorry. I'm beginning to think that anyone who could get caught up in this kind of adventure would hardly make a suitable wife for a man of my stature. I am disappointed.'

He made towards the door.

'Charles!' Faith made a move towards him.

'Don't try to stop me.'

'I won't,' she said. 'Charles, thank

you for coming. And, please, could I have my credit card?'

Charles took the card out of an inner pocket. 'I suppose you will need it,' he said savagely, 'to pay for this luxury accommodation of yours.'

'Oh, no,' Hannibal said quickly. 'Esperanza is quite right. Anna Lindstrom will be here in a day or two. But I know of a delightful villa at St Paul's bay where they are looking for someone to house-sit, if Faith is interested.'

Faith kept her eyes on his. 'I'm very interested. Goodbye, Charles.'

'You're mad, Fay,' Charles said, and with that went out, slamming the door.

★ ★ ★

It was a month later that Hannibal, Esperanza and Faith found themselves at the craft village in the centre of the island.

'I think you should choose yourself some jewellery,' Hannibal said, 'to celebrate your new appointment. Chief sales executive for the Mediterranean. Surely that deserves a little reward.'

She grinned at him happily. 'Yes, Brenda was very grateful.' She shook her head thoughtfully. 'I wonder where Laval went to? It was the last thing I expected — him running off like that.'

'Taking most of his fortune with him.' Hannibal said. 'All he seems to have left behind is empty buildings and bad debts. Oh, South America, I should think. And Veronique with him. He must have contacted her as soon as he knew the game was up. But that doesn't answer my question. What will you choose?'

'This necklace is pretty,' she said, holding up a delicate chain of beaten silver leaves.

'A ring would be prettier. Like the one Esperanza is wearing.'

Esperanza, who had never gained the confidence to say much in Faith's company, coloured prettily, and showed the diamond that sparkled on her finger.

'Do you think it quite proper,' Faith said, 'the new sales executive having such strong links with the sole licensee for import of Moonlight products into the island?'

'Oh, very proper,' Hannibal said, holding her so close that the elderly shopkeeper looked at them severely. 'Think of the saving in paperwork.'

'I'll believe you,' Faith said. 'My name is Faith, after all.'

'And mine is Hope,' Esperanza said unexpectedly. 'Faith and Hope, like the old planes over the island.'

'You know how they translate that now,' Hannibal asked, and his eyes were suddenly dark. 'Love, they say. Faith, Hope and Love.' Under the outraged eyes of the shopkeeper he bent and kissed Faith's lips. 'Now abideth Faith, Hope and Love, all three,' he said softly. 'And the greatest of these is Love.'